A Question of Time

by

Jamie Ashbird

Illustrated by

Janet Anderton

Improbable
PRESS

A SHERLOCKIAN ROMANCE

First published by Improbable Press in 2019

Improbable Press is an imprint of:
Clan Destine Press
www.clandestinepress.com.au
PO Box 121, Bittern
Victoria 3918 Australia

National Library of Australia Cataloguing-In-Publication data:

Ashbird, Jamie

A Question of Time

ISBN: 978-0-648 5236-6-6 (pb)
ISBN: 978-0-648 5236-7-3 (eb)

Illustrations © Janet Anderton
Cover © Willsin Rowe
Design & Typesetting: Clan Destine Press

Improbable Press
www.improbablepress.co.uk

Dedications

For much littler me – there's nothing wrong with being quiet. Anyone worth your time will be patient enough to wait for your voice to ring out.

Jamie Ashbird

For my mum, who rode her mobility scooter like a chariot from *Ben Hur*. Who listened when I said I wanted to be an artist, and trusted that I would be when I didn't. I miss you.

Janet Anderton

The stories you're about to read are precisely 221 words each, with the final word of every one beginning with B.

You'll no doubt have deduced that this idea was inspired by 221B Baker Street, the address of the world's first consulting detective.

This prose, and sometimes poetry, style is a unique and intriguing way to tell these tall tales and true, about a fine detective and his lovely doctor. Enjoy!

Atlin Merrick
Acquisitions Editor
Improbable Press

2085

'DAD COULD NEVER KEEP THAT LOOK OUT OF HIS EYE. IT WAS THERE WITH every word he spoke to Sherlock, even the angry ones – or mock anger depending on what Sherlock had broken that day. Every look was a love letter to his soulmate.

'And on behalf of Sherlock I will roll my eyes at the word *soulmate*. He preferred the ever-so-romantic: *mutual chemical attraction*.

'Though once, when he and I were drinking tequila shots under the kitchen table after my divorce, he called Dad – and this is true – his bestest forever friend.

'Sherlock could never hide it either, that look. Every scratch from a retort stand, every stain from an experiment, every bullet hole in the wall, those were love letters too. Uncalled for as they were.

'They were together until the end. And I'm thankful that neither left the other behind. Neither could have borne that pain.

'But now they've one last adventure, to nourish these trees, in whose shade people might find wisdom and kindness.

'Two elms, inosculated at their trunks, just as they were inosculated at their hearts. And yes, Sherlock bet me I couldn't fit inosculated into a eulogy – three times, Papa.

'The last words are theirs.

'From Dad: be brave, be kind, be true.

'From Sherlock: use your big words, always tell the bees.'

1810

'I MUST CONGRATULATE YOU, MR WATSON.'

Lady Margaret Renthwhistle hooked her arm through John's as he peered up at the stars.

'Whatever for, Lady Margaret?'

'Why, my dear, it is fifteen years today that you and Mr Holmes were acquainted.'

John's jaw wavered. 'I'm sure I don't—'

'Come, we're old friends. Do you imagine me an innocent? The way you look at him, and he you? Like two ravenous imps.'

'Madam, I assure you—'

'Ah look, there's Polly,' she interrupted, pointing down into the garden. 'And she has our bags.'

'Your chambermaid?'

'My chambermaid.'

John jerked out of her grip. 'But Mr Holmes is—'

'About to confront the lover my husband thinks stole the family jewels? Yes.'

A scream rang out from the ballroom beyond the balcony doors.

'Best see to your man, Mr Watson.'

John cried out as Lady Renthwhistle leapt off the low balcony and ran into Polly's arms.

'Tell Mr Renthwhistle he can spend every deuced minute at the club now.' And with a wave she and Polly dissolved into the night.

John raced back indoors to find Sherlock grappling with Lady Renthwhistle's innocent lover. After pulling them apart and whispering in Sherlock's ear, he helped both men off the floor. With lavish apologies and a nod to Mr Renthwhistle, they scarpered hand in hand from the ballroom.

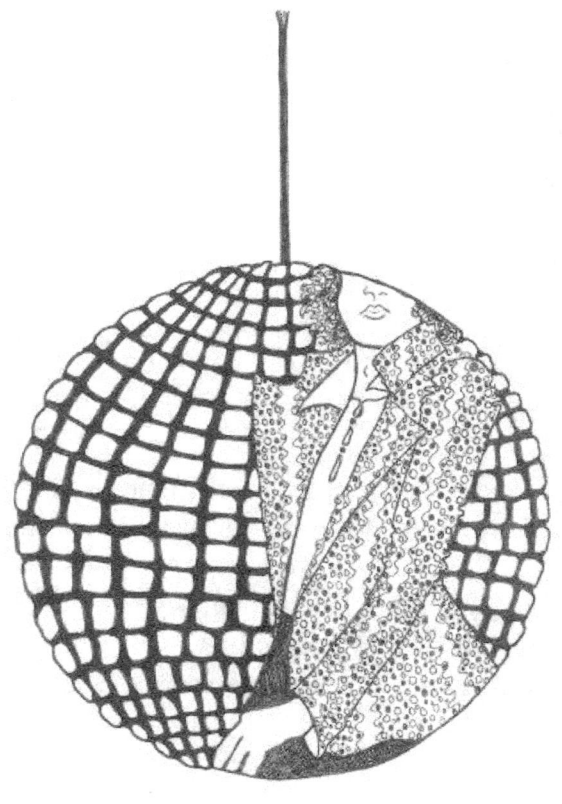

1973

'NOT SO MUCH THE GREAT DETECTIVE NOW, EY?'

The speakers in Crackers pumped out The Temptations while the magic of the dark room was chased away by the harsh fluorescent lights. The patrons had gone from dancing to cowering from the man with the gun.

Sherlock, his hands up, exhaled sharply. 'I'd heard you were an interesting case.'

'You what?'

'But here you are being quite obvious. Shame, really.'

'I should gag you.'

'Wise idea.' Sherlock's eyes flickered behind to a man in a plum corduroy suit crawling slowly toward them. *A soldier? No civilian moved like that. Tanned, perhaps returned from Dhofar.*

'Bet you'd love that, you deviant. Why you dressed like a disco ball?'

'I'm considering a career change to decorative ceiling ornament.'

Without taking his eyes off the gunman Sherlock watched the soldier move closer in his periphery. A quick glance and Sherlock saw his signal. *Keep him busy.*

'Well? Are you going to gag me or tell me what it is you want?'

'I want,' the man barked out. But what he wanted remained a mystery as the soldier surged. He grabbed the gun, twisted the gunman's arm back, and forced him to the floor.

'Thank you.'

'You're welcome.'

'Sherlock Holmes.'

'John Watson.'

They shook hands, neither letting go. Eyes gleamed as polite smiles turned to beams.

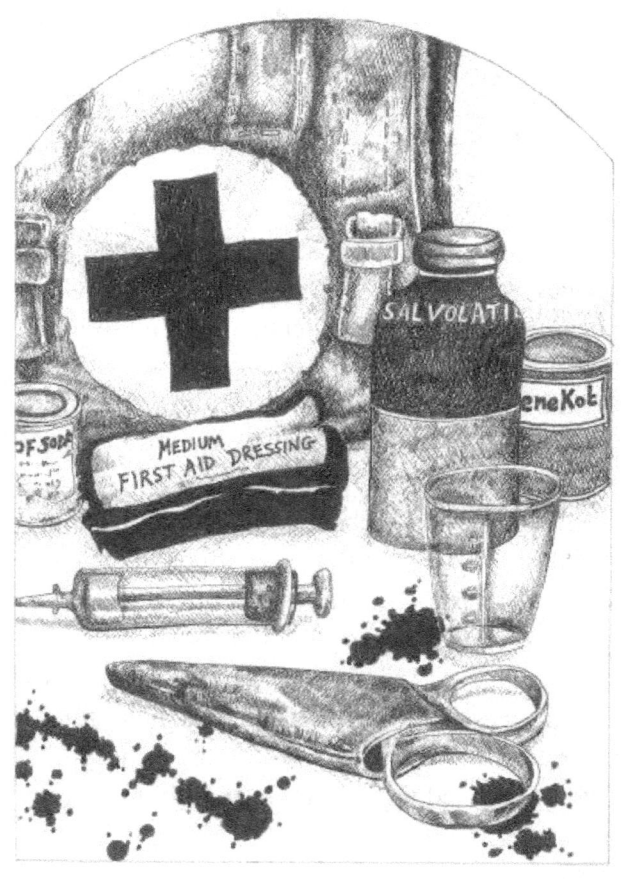

1917

'YOU'LL NOT GO BACK, WATSON. DO YOU HEAR?' SHERLOCK DRAPED himself blanket-like over John, head resting on his chest.

'The army doesn't need broken soldiers, dear boy.' John brushed the hair from Sherlock's face while slender fingers played with the bandages across John's shoulder.

Sherlock scrambled to his elbows, a scowl storming across his sharp features, the bedframe complaining.

'They're desperate now. They'll take anyone. They'll take you, too, the moment your bandages are off.'

John burst into a hearty laugh.

'Shall we run away then, my love? Hmm?' He ran a hand down Sherlock's neck.

'Where to?' Sherlock pouted like a child.

'Norway. Let's secrete ourselves in a fjord and solve cases of stolen sheep and burgled brunost.'

Sherlock tapped along John's ribs and with a grin of dark mischief wriggled down between his legs. His fingers followed after him, along chest, belly, twisting in fine hair, circling, fluttering, teasing fattening flesh.

'Capital idea, Watson, but I've a fjord right here I'm aching to explore.'

His fingers delved between John's legs, stroking, pushing, begging admittance.

With one hand still pressing and circling, Sherlock took John's cock in the other, leant in to kiss the member's leaking head and slid his grip along warm silky skin.

John tipped his head back with a peaceful sigh. 'You are truly brilliant, my boy.'

1567

I WROTE A SONNET FOR MY SWEETHEART. SUCH SLENDER CONSIDERATION
he gives to my dabbles in the arts, but can conceive of none better
in the art of love. Look here:

Upon a dreary night of mud and rain
My love and I by a hedgerow crouch down
By foot and by steed our prey didst we gain
In the cold mud there did our bodies drown

'Hark there, do you see?' My love did proclaim
'The footprints, look there, the blaze on his horse
For theft of the jewels that man is to blame'
'Then why,' said I, 'do we dwell in this gorse?'

The inn door we did not hear clang shut
'Fore the woman's voice rung clear and said
'Come out now, Sherlock Holmes, 'ere you I cut'
'Dear John,' my love said, 'I fear I'm misled'

I did not, could not, think of my love less
When he bowed low and said, 'Long live Queen Bess'

He tells me I should not bestrew his errors about the city, but
Her Majesty – desiring it to be known she outwitted Sir Sherlock
Holmes – insists.

Deny it he will but he preens like a proud cock to see his name in
print. I am determined to publish with all speed in *The Foreshore
Pamphlet* and sign it: To My Beau.

1895

A SLOW DRIP OF HEAVY DROPS FELL FROM THE HOTHOUSE CEILING ONTO THE two men below.

'I hardly expected it to happen like this,' Watson whispered, a hair's breadth from Holmes's mouth.

'You've been imagining it?'

'Oh, yes. On the rooftops of the city, breathless after a chase. At the foot of our own stairs at Baker Street, breathless after a chase. In the back of a cab—'

'Breathless after a chase? I detect a pattern to these whimsies of yours, John.'

'Hardly fanciful. We spend half our days out of breath at the heels of some nefarious criminal.'

'True. Oh!' Holmes beamed as a giant swallowtail fluttered by.

'You shine, you know, when you're on a case. You're like a beacon.'

'So I recall from your sensational accounts of our adventures. I didn't imagine us to be breathless.'

'Ho ho! You've been imagining too?'

Holmes leaned in and brushed his lips against John's.

'Of course, though not so adventurous as you. At home, in our own rooms. A fire lit, a pot of tea. A pipe for me, a brandy for you. Comfortable, warm.'

'You old sop. And you accuse me of being a romantic.'

'Hardly, my dear. If I were I'd have thought of this sooner.'

And they kissed for the very seventh time surrounded by orchids and butterflies.

47 BCE

'GAIUS ARTURUS, WELCOME.'

The man hesitated in the darkened doorway.

'Enter. Despite rumours there are no vengeful spirits here, I've not angered the gods. It is impossible to anger something that doesn't exist.'

Gaius gasped, horrified. He staggered out and ran back down the road.

Soft footsteps entered the dark room, a bowl of fresh berries was clunked onto the table.

'Who was that?'

A languid hand flapped, barely illuminated by the light from the doorway.

'Pah, no one. A ghost, Johannes.'

Johannes tutted and fussed, opening up the shuttered window. 'That better not have been a client. We're down to our last five sestertii.'

He turned around. 'Oh for– It's high noon, put some clothes on. You're indecent,' he said, with absolutely no conviction.

An utterly bare Sherlock rolled over on his couch. One bent leg slowly followed the other to expose everything to Johannes.

'First, that man has lost his prized fighting dog – I'd rather help a murderer.

'Second, I have a denarius or two squirrelled away, and third,' Sherlock ran his fingers in an airy light pitter patter from hips to collarbones, 'my clothes are itchy.'

Johannes drew closer, pulled by an invisible thread.

'And to think you Romans call *us* uncivilised.'

Sherlock's face split into an enormous grin. 'Then what are you waiting for? Invade me, you barbarian.'

2017

'WE CAN'T LOITER INSIDE A SCULPTURE ALL DAY, SHERLOCK.'

'...and the drones are often tightly–'

'There's a small child tying your shoelaces together.'

'On the other hand, *Anthidium manicatum*–'

'I wonder how many selfies we've been in the background of today? We'll be a hashtag by now. Hashtag DickAndDocInTheHive.'

'...but when you take into account the humble honeybee–'

'And when you were ear-to-the-floor, arse-in-the-air this morning? That'll be on Instagram. 'Spotted these two in The Hive at Kew Gardens today.' Heart emoji, magnifying glass, eggplant.'

'Of course *Bombus humilis* wouldn't be seen dead on a–'

'There's a chill in the air now. It's a bit chilly. I'm chilly. Are you chilly?'

'...and it is odd that no one ever–'

'The gardens close in an hour, Sherlock. I've seen the inside of the loo and the inside of this beehive.'

'...plus, if you think about it, society would be better off if we took lessons–'

'I guess you could lie here all day, as we've just proven, but that's not to say we haven't annoyed everyone, including those five school groups.'

'...the synergy, John. The downright majesty of a well-formed–'

'That volunteer has been glaring at us for the last three hours, you know.'

'...and if, *if* I believed in reincarnation, which is a ludicrous fairytale, I'd come back as a bumblebee.'

1952

'THE BROAD HAD GAMS AS TALL AS THE HOOVER DAM.'

'John. Stop it.' Sherlock flattened himself against the cold brick wall with a pistol loaded and ready.

'She was deadly, like a clip joint full of rattlesnakes,' John drawled from a tight jaw. He tipped the brim of his hat low over his eyes.

'Really, now?' Sherlock glanced back. 'This is a serious investigation.'

'Her name was trouble. The kind that walked around in stilettos and wasn't afraid to kick a fella right in the unmentionables. The broad didn't have a lick of sense but she sure had the spondulix to hire a sleuth.'

'What's gotten into you?' Sherlock took a swift peek around the corner.

'Lucky for her, the greatest private dick in town was on the job, along with his faithful assistant Doctor Long John.'

'In *town?*'

'The greatest private dick in the *world* was on the job.'

'No more detective movies, John. They're no good. You've gone all doolally.'

'He also had the best privates and the greatest dick.'

Sherlock blinked in confusion for a moment, took a peek around the wall again. 'That makes no sense but you may proceed, and once we've caught this grifter we're going home. I'll let you investigate the greatest private dick in the world if you play your cards right, baby.'

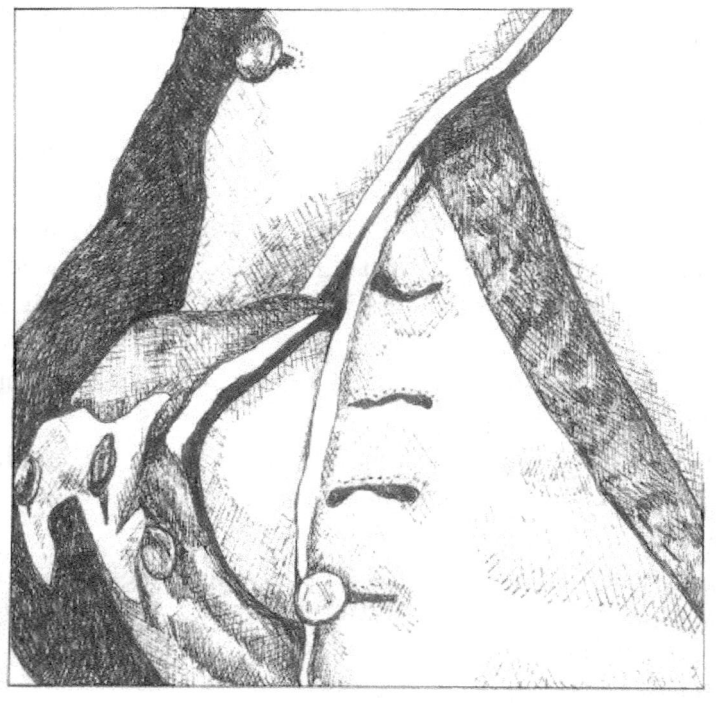

1816

'DON'T CALL IT THAT, SHERLOCK, I BEG OF YOU.'

'Come now, John, Old Boney only wants to say how do.'

'And I shall greet him with good cheer but if you persist with the name Old Boney I shall be warming my bed instead of yours.'

'Ah, but my Old Boney is much prettier and by all accounts much taller than Old Emperor Boney-parte. See here his rosy complexion?'

'It's with thanks to *that* Old Boney that I returned to England half an invalid.'

'Awful man. I've a mind to go off and give him what for for injuring my own precious John.'

'You mock me, you rogue.'

'Not at all, my dear. But here, look.' Sherlock gripped his Boney and gave it a waggle. 'You have a chance to punish my Old Boney. He needs a good thrashing and you are the very man to do it.'

John growled and moved like a whirlwind to straddle Sherlock's long bare legs. 'A thrashing? I hardly think that would be sufficient for such a tyrant.'

'No?' Sherlock huffed as John rolled his hips.

'Oh, no. I've a much more punishing ordeal in mind. Brace yourself.' John leant in to murmur in his darling's ear. 'This won't hurt, much.'

Every inch of Sherlock's skin quivered at those words, hummed in his love's baritone.

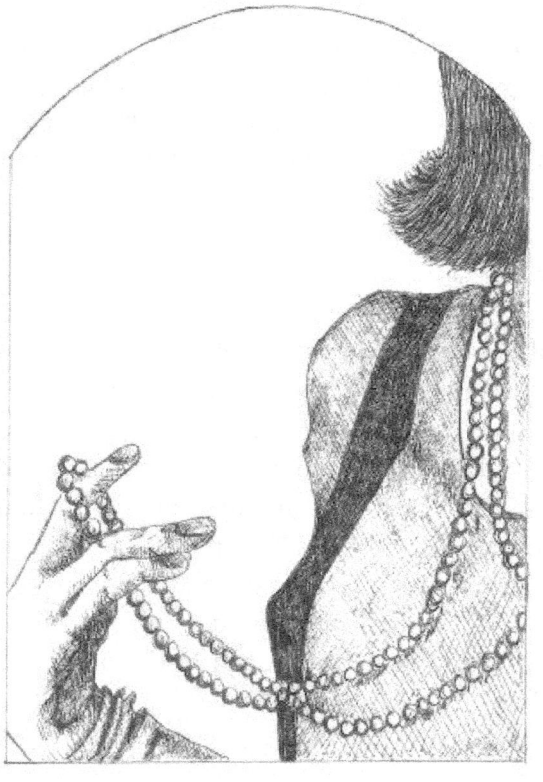

1929

'CAN'T SAY I UNDERSTOOD A WORD HE SAID. YOU MUST DO, DOCTOR Watson, being a genius yourself?' said Barbara Dalrymple.

'Me? No.' John Watson blushed and shooed away the compliment.

'I say, do you know what would be rather splendid? If you came down to Dalrymple House. Daddy won't mind at all.'

'Well, I–'

'Do you shoot? You can shoot all you like there. Must be the season for something or other. Whatever it is, there'll be enough about.'

'Yes. No, but–'

'Roderick Montalbert Fitzlexington is throwing a frightful shindig tomorrow. You ought to come, Johnny – may I call you Johnny? – make sure I don't get too blotto.'

John looked to Sherlock, his eyes sending distress signals.

Sherlock left Gregson and came to his darling's aid, leaning in close. 'All right, old chap?'

John clutched his arm.

'Was telling old Johnny I didn't understand a word you said, Mr Holmes. It's quite the mystery.'

Sherlock placed his hand in the small of John's back. 'Shall I slow it down for you, Miss Dalrymple? You murdered your entire household, including the gardener, you're quite mad, and Gregson over there will arrest you shortly.'

'I say, you're a grim sort of fellow, ain't you? What do you say to that party, Johnny?'

John hooked his arm around Sherlock's. 'I'm happily spoken for, Babs.'

1348

PART 1

I DID NOT KNOW LONELINESS UNTIL THERE WAS NO ONE LEFT TO HEAR MY voice. I have nothing. No one. All I have are memories I would gladly give away, and a life I am not prepared to let go of.

Last Wednesday, that's when little Wiggins died.

My entire village is gone. I should've died too, I should've joined my Mary and be done with it. Now I tramp my way, praying I am not alone in the world.

Another village looms dark and still in the evening light. I think to find a house to sleep in that is not someone's tomb. There is not a movement to be seen, not a sound, but that's when I see the faint glow of firelight from beneath a door.

That is where I find him, pale as the figure of death that sits at his head, waiting, alone. Dark bruises ring his eyes. He has no rash I can see, only the wicked buboes, one upon his fevered neck, the other in the crease of his thigh – that one burst and bleeding.

I sit beside him, laying my cool hand upon his heated brow, as I had done with so many others. At my touch the man gasps deep. I watch his chest deflate again and wait for his next breath.

1368

PART 2

TWO POTS OF HONEY I COLLECTED THIS WEEK. JOHN WILL BE PLEASED. AND if Mrs Hudson fires her oven, as she said she would, I shall make us fresh loaves. Then I can wake John with a warm bit of bread covered in honey – his favourite thing.

He will blink his eyes open and smack his lips. Then he will roll onto his back, stretch himself and yawn the sort of yawn made by small woodland creatures, not grown men. After that he will blink his pretty eyes at me and smile a soft smile. The same smile I first saw when I awakened from the very nearly dead.

I will kiss him then, all quiet and soft in the morning because, though I could try, why would I resist?

Then I will break off a piece of honeyed bread and place it into my honey's mouth. He will lick my sticky fingers clean because we shall not waste sweets and we will do this until all the bread is gone.

Then, as he always does, he will grumble his way to sitting, throw his arms around my neck and kiss my nose, my lips, and the scar where my bubo once was. And we will sit wrapped around each other in the morning light, counting the waves of our breaths.

1997

OF COURSE THAT WAS THE COSTUME SHERLOCK PICKED OUT FOR ME. BLONDE pigtails and a short white dress. He always loved Baby best.

With a body like his I'd have sworn he'd go as Posh – how better to show off those legs than a tiny black dress? Well, with a tiny sequined Union Jack dress instead.

I appreciated his Ginger more and more the faster we ran and the higher that dress rose, until we finally caught Jenkins and called Lestrade to come take him in. And then I pulled my Ginger Spice into a dead-end alley and took him against the grimy damp brick wall.

Neither the running nor the taking against a wall are easy things to do in ten-inch platforms, but with some luck, some balance, and a little bit of girl power, we did it.

I rucked that dress right up to his armpits, unsurprised by the lacy black knickers beneath. My Sherlock was thorough when it came to his disguises.

I pulled the lace aside and with hardly a warning, pushed right in. I set a pace to the beat of *Spice Up Your Life* and gripped his hips so hard I found my hand prints there later that night.

Once the alley was thoroughly spiced we danced home hand in hand, Ginger Spice and Baby.

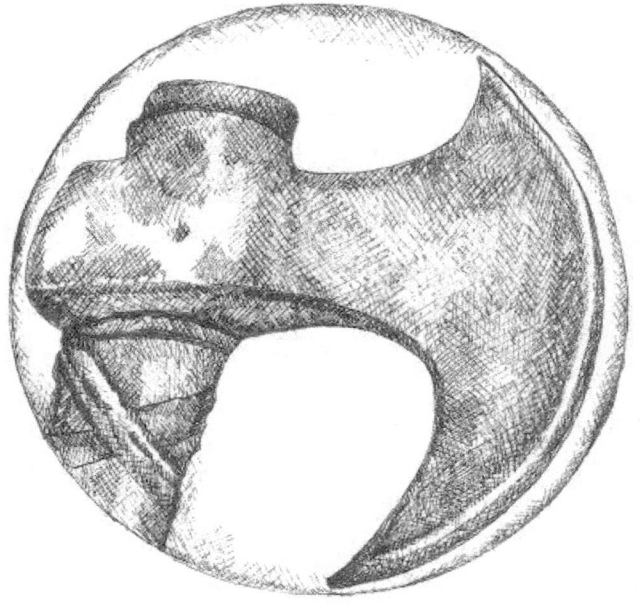

1086

'ONE EWE.'

'Wuuuun… yoooooo.' The assessor scratched with his quill.

'Three pigs.'

'Threeeeee… pigs.'

'One– Oh!'

'What? What is it?'

'One angry man. One very angry man. One very naked, very angry-looking man. With a sword. And an axe.'

'Wuuuuun… verrrry… angrrrr…'

'What are you–? Stop writing and run! He's coming right for us.'

'We're not finished accounting yet.'

'Sherlock!' The angry naked man burst through the door.

A pile of blankets in the corner shifted and suddenly there was one angry naked man and one sleepy naked man staring at the intruders.

The assessor held his quill out like a knife. 'We've been charged by his Majesty, King William, to take account of his kingdom. For taxes and whatnot!'

'John?' Sherlock rubbed at his half-lidded eyes.

'Go back to bed, beloved. I'll take care of this.' John handed Sherlock the axe and swung the sword. With teeth bared and a low growl, he advanced.

'Well, we're done here.' The two assessors backed out. 'We'll be away. Thank you, gentlemen.'

At the threshold they both turned and ran without stopping for breath until they were sure the mad Saxon with the sword wasn't after them.

'So, a ewe, three pigs, two villagers, one or both of them quite mad, and I had a look round the back. Are we counting beehives?'

1666

'THE WHOLE HOUSE, MRS HUDSON, BURNT?'

'Oh, yes, Mrs Turner. And I in my night gown these two days with nought else to wear. You ought have seen the people running about like mad creatures. 'T'was a lamentable spectacle.'

'I heard the king's own baker down Puddin' Lane started it. The king himself came out to help, I heard.'

'He never did. The king awake before dinner? And besides it wasn't the baker, it was Mr Holmes.'

'No.'

'Indeed it was. I always said, didn't I, that he'd burn the house down one day. Well, he's done it now, and taken half the city with it.'

'Is he well, the dear sweet boy? And Mr Watson?'

'Don't sweet boy him. Mr Holmes's brother instructed Mr Watson to take him into the country for a spell lest he find himself at the end of a rope. Poor Mr Watson was furious.'

'Doctor Watson is a dear man. And mighty pretty.'

'Indeed he is, Mrs Turner, and brave, too. Never have I seen a man so determined. He threw himself into the flames after Mr Holmes. I thought he'd surely perished, but by and by out he came, Mr Holmes with him.'

'Mr Holmes will surely languish in the country with nought to divert him.'

'As he brews, Mrs Turner, let him bake.'

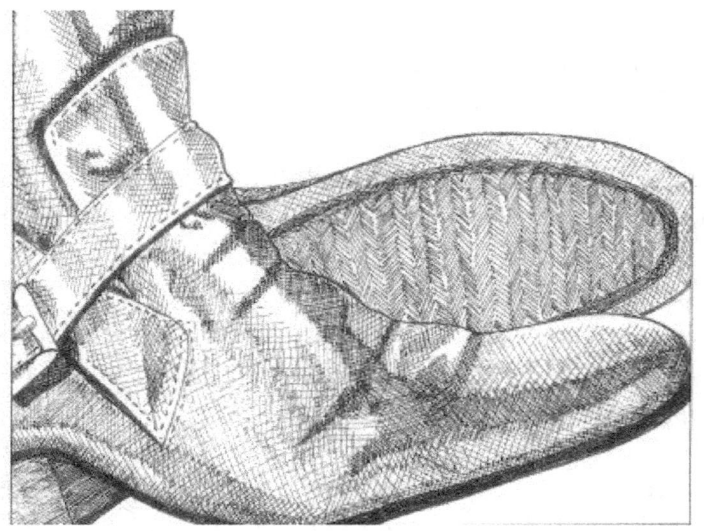

1962

'YOU KNOW I ADORE YOU, SHERLOCK, YES?'

A harrumph from the face buried in the pillowcase.

'I love you beyond all reckoning.'

A hum and a clench of bare arse cheeks.

'But I am not getting undressed in this weather.'

A grumble.

John wrapped his scarf tighter. 'I'll fetch more coal tomorrow. I've asked the Hudson about central heating six times this fortnight.'

Silence.

'Please, babe, put something on. Come open the rest of your presents, I'll warm up some mulled wine.'

Nothing but the wiggle of a pert backside.

'My sweet,' John bent and gave a soft peck to both cheeks, 'I can't feel my fingers, m'not exposing my todger to a chill.'

A gathering of knees to chest and a lifting of a tail bone.

'I know. I dig what you're saying, it'll be warmed up right away but I swear, it's all my blood can do to keep my heart pumping, let alone that.'

A moan and a sinuous roll onto a pale back. Dark eyes blinking a slow wave, a glint of mischief. Long thin fingers trailing down down bare chest through crisp short hair to curl around hard flesh.

'If I die of pneumonia, I'm coming back as a coughing ghost.' John sighed, utterly resigned. 'Happy Christmas, Holmes.' He stripped off every layer, including his boots.

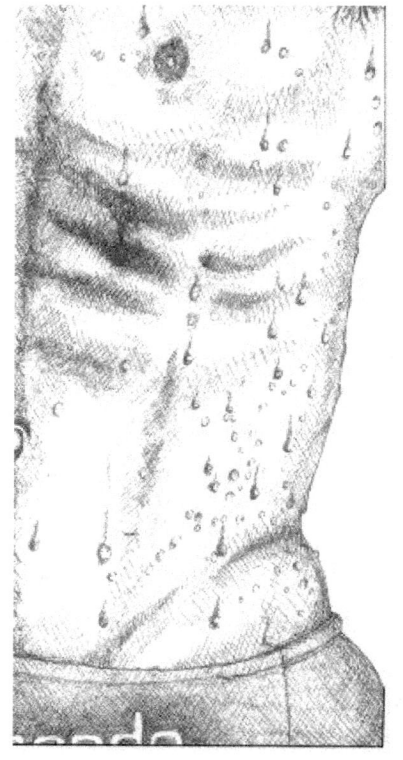

2012

I SHOULD HAVE NOTICED WHEN HE SCUTTLED PAST WITHOUT QUIPPING ABOUT the nest I'd built in front of the telly. He'd had so much to say during the opening ceremony after all. At the very least he could have slowed down so I could make my coxless pairs joke.

I should have paid attention when I heard tapping and scratching behind his door but he makes weird noises all the time, and then Gemma Gibbons won the silver in judo and I forgot.

The puppy food in the fridge should have tipped me off, but he's Sherlock. I've found everything from mud-filled balloons to eyeballs.

Turns out by the 9th he wasn't even hiding anymore. They walked right past me. Twice. But Jade Jones had just won gold and I was annoyed. He'd promised we'd watch the boxing together, but was nowhere to be found when Nicola Adams won. I didn't speak to him for the next two days.

I heard yapping on the 11th, but Tom Daley was diving and, well…Tom Daley. I had a moment.

It took Sherlock placing a wriggling puppy in my lap to get the point across. I was watching Anthony Joshua beat Cammarelle but being nuzzled by a bouncy Staffie and a happy detective was better than any gold. We called her Basketball.

1969

[July 20 13:20] Man opposite excitable today. Flicking between BBC 1 and ITV. TV visible when wind blows curtains in.

[July 20 17:43] Man keeps adjusting his telescope. Shook fist at sky. May be slightly mad.

[July 20 20:31] Whooping outside. Children in tinfoil hats. Man opposite inspecting noise. Spotted me, gave two thumbs up and giant grin. Is certainly mad. (Angle of thumbs indicates doctor.)

[July 21 01:17] Window across closed. He is still awake. Comparing his TV light flicker pattern to mine he is on BBC1, occasional changes to ITV. Checks sky every 10-15 minutes.

[July 21 02:35] He's still awake. Why am I?

[July 21 02:48] He keeps checking sky. Must know he won't see men on the moon, even without clouds. *He keeps looking!*

[July 21 03:10] Caught me looking. I should not have fallen asleep, face smashed against window, binoculars in hand.

[July 21 03:49] Broadcast says it's happening. Find I don't care to watch anything other than him.

[July 21 03:50] Man waving for attention. Didn't notice I was already staring at him. He only came to press hand to glass a moment.

[July 21 03:56] Man may be crying.

[July 21 04:11] Man at window. Not looking at sky. Looking at me. Smiling like a lunatic. Quite unbidden, find I am smiling back.

1920

What Lurks at the Bottom of the Garden?

A MR SHERLOCK HOLMES OF LONDON HAS DISMISSED THE ASTONISHING photographs of Miss Wright and Miss Griffith of Cottingley and their dancing fairy creatures as a hoax. The girls themselves he calls pathological liars who, without intervention, have the capacity to become hardened fraudsters if they continue to be indulged in their charade, which has caused quite the sensation here and abroad.

Mr Holmes spoke of his amazement that any sensible person could look upon the photographs and see anything other than flat cardboard cutouts of obviously drawn figures with very poor shading and attempts to convey motion.

Mr Arthur Conan Doyle, renowned author and friend to the spiritualist movement, is currently touring Australia. He continues to champion the Cottingley girls and devotes much energy into the investigation to prove the authenticity of the photographs.

When asked what he thought of the efforts of Mr Doyle and others, Mr Holmes quipped that Mr Doyle was welcome to waste his own time and money on fantasies as he saw fit.

Mr Watson, close friend and confidant of Mr Holmes, took his companion's arm and interrupted what looked to become a lengthy lecture by Mr Holmes. As they departed, Mr Holmes took a parting volley at Mr Doyle calling his efforts 'a load of bollocks'.

1703

SUCH MISFORTUNES BEFELL ENGLAND DURING THAT GREAT STORM. TREES were felled, ships blown to Sweden, a cascade of toppled chimneys about London.

By such a chimney Mr Sherlock Holmes and I dug away bricks to free the corpse that lay beneath.

'Tis is a terrible calamity, Mr Holmes.' Mrs Farnell sniffed, her eyes rimmed red. 'My dearest husband, pressed like a flower.'

Mr Holmes observed, as did I, that Mrs Farnell fretted too much with the shawl about her neck and her dark eyes darted everywhere but the body of her husband.

I kicked at the shards of a broken vase and noted the purple aconite. 'Like a flower, yes. Or like you poisoning him by putting monkshood in his food, Mrs Farnell.' I said.

Mrs Farnell gaped. 'You accuse me, sir?'

'I wonder that you presaged your chimney would fall,' said Mr Holmes, 'or was the storm an advantageous miracle given your failed attempt to burn him three days ago?'

He pulled the shawl from her neck to reveal livid marks left by choking fingers, freshly made, not yet yellowing.

'My sympathies, Mrs Farnell. Your husband must have been a fearsome brute,' I murmured.

She collapsed to her knees and hid her head in her hands.

'I fear, Madam,' Mr Holmes said, 'you have an engagement at the Old Bailey.'

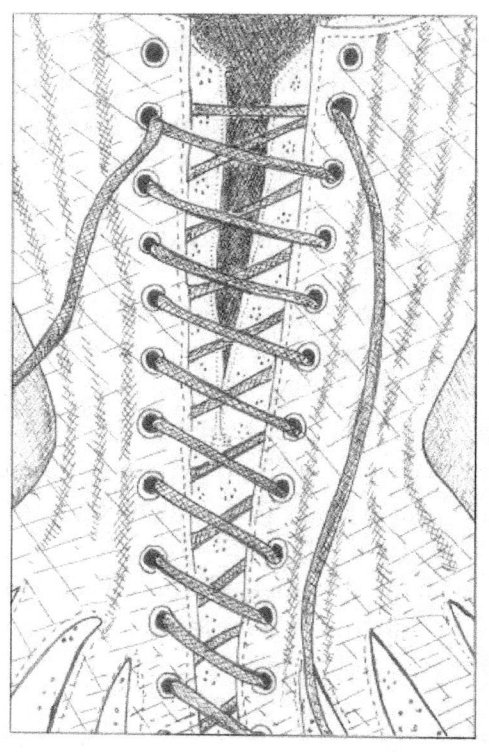

1761

'BE STILL, AND BREATHE OUT.'

'I am, I have.'

'Breathe out more.' John tugged at the laces of the stays.

'I've nothing left to breathe out.'

'Well then, bend over.'

Sherlock laughed. 'You tempt me but–'

'To tie you off, imp.' John slapped the swell of Sherlock's bottom below the stiff fabric.

'Still.' Sherlock threw a smirk over his shoulder.

'There.' John pulled to test his handiwork before dropping to his knees. 'Now, your petticoats.' He steadied the columns of Sherlock's legs as he stepped into pool after pool of silk and linen.

'You'll be the belle of the ball.' John's hands lingered at the top of Sherlock's thighs, petticoats bunched on his forearms.

Sherlock ran a finger along John's upturned jaw. 'Never fear, my sweet, I've only eyes for you.'

He tipped his head at John's raised eyebrow. 'And the assassin come to kill Lord Thrushthwaite, of course. Though I prefer you.'

'You are kind.'

'I am.'

'You will be careful?'

'But you're so careful for me.'

'Still,' with his clever fingers John strapped a knife to Sherlock's thigh, 'you'll not stray from my sight.'

'No, sir.'

To Sherlock's other thigh he strapped a pistol. 'And you'll not go off at half cock.'

'Care to make that a certainty?'

John slipped himself beneath Sherlock's skirts. 'Consider it done, my beauty.'

1892

'BECAUSE IT'S TREASON,' JOHN HISSED THROUGH HIS TEETH.

'To solve a crime?'

'To suggest that…' John looked over h:s shoulder, running a nervous hand over his moustache. He leaned c_oser. 'That her Majesty herself may have ordered these atrocities.'

'I suggested nothing of the sort. I merely suggest that it seems awfully convenient that a murderer who seems to relish in his killings should all of a sudden stop once the final link in a sordid chain has been broken.'

John made a disbelieving grunt which delighted Sherlock, who clapped his hands together with an enormous grin.

'You do make me work hard to convince you, dear boy.' His eyes glinted and his grin grew shark-like. 'Perhaps you can work me even harder tonight.'

John Watson tutted and rolled his eyes. 'Five women are dead.'

'Yes,' Sherlock said. 'And the trail that leads to the illegitimate child of a royal prince is destroyed.'

'And you suggest a royal conspiracy?'

Sherlock threw his hands up in frustration. 'It's perfectly logical. All the circumstances point toward it.'

'And you punned at me to suggest a night of debauchery.'

Sherlock sobered. 'Well, alright. Perhaps that was out of order.'

'You're right, I should work you harder.' John tapped his chin. 'And if I'm feeling generous I shall let you work me hard right back.'

1731

NOT SINCE THAT MONK, CENTURIES AGO, USED MY SPINE TO PROP UP AN obscene scribble while he had his way with a postulant have I seen such blatant disregard for my kind.

Now two barbarians are stacking my friends so the taller one can take a closer look at the old emperor above us.

'More light,' the taller one says.

The shorter one raises his candle. 'Is it him?' he asks.

'Yes. Vitellius.'

'My clever husband,' the shorter one says and then, with no warning, leans in and kisses his companion's backside.

The taller one, crying out in surprise, jerks his hips forward and rattles my shelf in a most violent manner. He windmills his arms and falls, knocking the candle from his friend's grip before toppling them both to the floor.

The knock has old Vitellius rocking about until he, too, falls, smashing to the ground. The two fools shake themselves off and scrabble through the broken pottery.

'It's not here,' I hear them mutter, and then off they go. Not a thought to cleaning up or noticing the smoke drifting from the bottom of the curtains. Smoke…fire. FIRE!

Those unconscionable devils. Fetch the buckets. Fetch the Bailiff. Fetch me a brandy. I can do nought but gather my pages and hold my *Judith* and *Beowulf* tight between my boards.

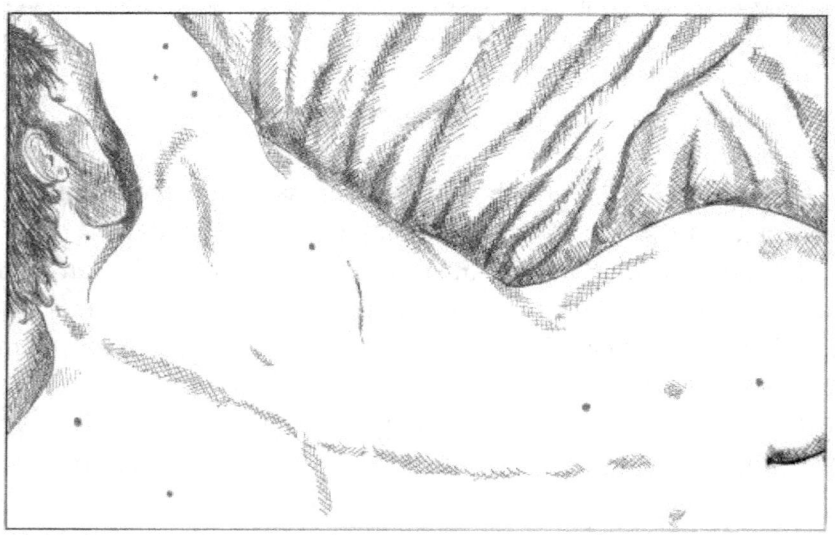

1629

'HERE.' SHERLOCK'S BREATH BLEW HOT BEHIND JOHN'S EAR. 'AND HERE.' He played his fingers soft-slow along the scars on John's hand. 'And here.' He traced a mole near John's hairline. 'Covered in devil's marks, you witch,' he whispered into John's neck.

John stiffened. 'The fault is yours, with your braziers and crucibles. Anywhere I wish to set down a plate I am thwarted by your detritus. That I am not marked all over is beyond comprehension.'

Sherlock drew back. 'You are quarrelsome today. What ails you?'

With a heavy sigh John turned away to sit by the fire. 'The child. We never did find her.'

'And today the witch hangs.'

'You said I had a mark and I...'

Sherlock went to him, sitting in his own chair opposite. 'Forgive me. It was said in jest.' He placed a hand on John's knee.

'I know it.' John set his hand on Sherlock's. 'But as certain as the tide ebbs and flows that unfortunate wretch must hang, and here we sit. Lord, what evil befell that child?'

'Good god!' Sherlock leapt to his feet, clasped John's face in two hands and kissed him hard.

'The tides. The child is in the caves, dear man. You've shone your light on the crux again. Come, we may yet save that woman and her bairn.'

1315

'BROTHER JOHN, THIS IS BROTHER SHERLOCK.' ABBOT MICHAEL GESTURED at a sharp man who was watching John over steepled hands.

'He's come from St Saviour to see our infirmary. To record healing practices around the country.'

He turned to Sherlock. 'Brother John will provide you with everything you need.' Abbot Michael gave a nod and went on his way.

'Are you a medical man yourself, brother?' John continued inspecting his patient's bandages. He looked up to see the strange man striding down the infirmary, peering intently at the faces of every patient. John hurried after him.

'Is there something I can help you with?'

'No.' Brother Sherlock squinted at every face until he stopped beside a bed and wheeled around, bumping chests with John, who, it turned out, blushed a very pretty shade of pink. 'Have you a pin?' Sherlock asked.

John shook his head.

'I'll improvise then.' Sherlock spun around and gave a great thump to the patient's chest.

'Have you lost your senses?' John shouted, reaching out to grab Sherlock's arm.

At the same moment the patient shot upright with a yelp.

Upon seeing Sherlock his eyes widened and, not caring a jot for his nakedness, pushed the blankets aside and ran off.

Sherlock started after him, looking back at John as he went. 'Care for an adventure, brother?'

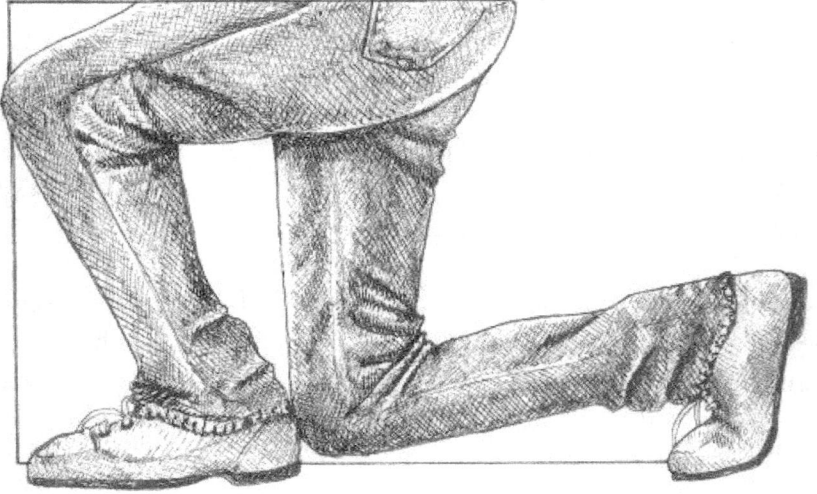

2014

I can't believe this is our in. You think the kidnapper is a sensual masseur?

It's just a bit of tantric massage, John. What could possibly go wrong?

I don't know, I leave you for the random guy with magic hands that elicit a mind blowing full body orgasm?

That's not funny, John.

Is a bit.

Hmm.

Appointment's at 3. I'll wait outside the pub. Opposite the park.

On my way.

There's a wedding on.

Mazel tov.

Cars everywhere. You're better off walking.

Ok.

It's two ladies.

Ladies, John? Ladies? Are you from the 50s?

You're making jokes now? Good boy. Are you laughing at yourself as well?

It was funny.

That's not really your call, darling. Great though isn't it? About time everyone was allowed to be happy.

Are you saying you're not happy? You need a document and vows to be content in life?

I didn't say that. What's the matter with you? I said it's lovely and it's about time. I'm making no other statements.

If you feel a piece of paper legitimises our relationship in your mind, John, I'll give you a piece of paper. If that's what will make you happy.

I am happy. Stop putting words in my mouth. Forget it. Where are you?

'Right behind you, John.'
'Why are you kneel– Oh. You bastard.'

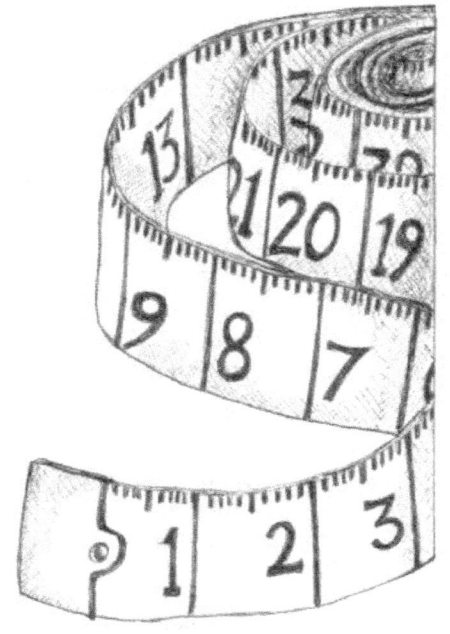

1993

JOHN SQUINTED AT THE SIGHT BELOW THEM. 'I COUNT TWENTY AT LEAST.'

Sherlock mouthed a low whistle around his unlit cigarette. 'How many of them can you handle?'

'This is for the case?'

'Yep.'

John plucked the cigarette from Sherlock's mouth, crushed it in his hand. 'I can take twelve, easy.'

Sherlock peered down, unconvinced. 'You sure?'

John tutted. 'Don't sound so surprised. You know I've done my fair share.'

Sherlock grunted his admiration.

'You? Think you can take the rest of them?'

Sherlock flicked his dark hair from his face, reached for the cigarette hidden behind his ear and tucked it into his mouth. 'Yeah. But you go first.'

John picked up the long log of glittery pink silicone from the bed, ran a finger along detailed veins. 'We could always get a smaller one.'

Sherlock sucked on his cigarette, scowled as he remembered it was unlit. 'No. This is the exact model found on–'

'In.'

'Yes, *in* the victims.' Sherlock spat the cigarette onto the floor, to unimpressed tutting. 'It's scientific analysis, John. Every parameter must be considered. Every act perfectly recreated.'

'If you say so.'

Side by side they stared awhile at the double-ended, twenty-inch dildo between them.

John climbed off the bed with a resigned sigh.

'You get undressed, sweet-cheeks. I'll fetch the lube and the bath-towels.'

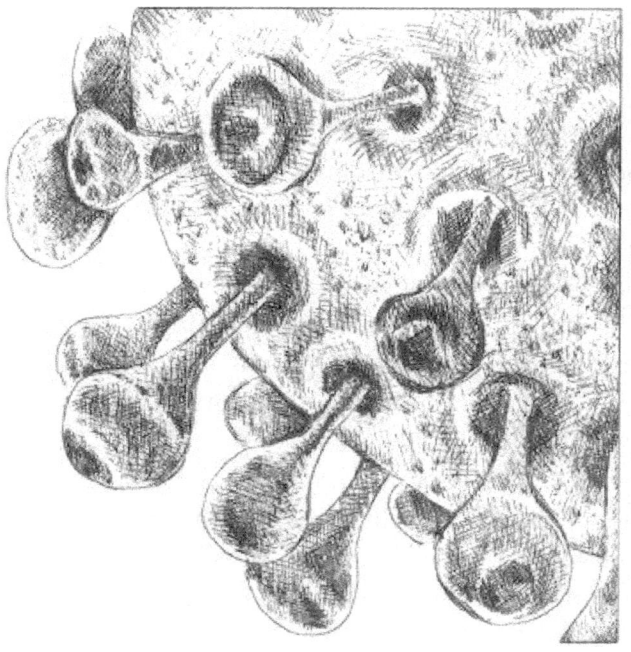

1987

I'D NEVER SEEN SHERLOCK SO NERVOUS. MAYBE ONCE, BEFORE HIS FIRST concert at the Royal Albert Hall, but not before and not since.

The clinic's waiting room was the size of a matchbox but that hadn't stopped him pacing.

Perhaps that was a good thing. I couldn't have stopped myself holding his hand and we already had the suspicious glares from other patients. No one wants a scuffle at the doctor's office.

We'd all been bombarded with the terrifying adverts. The bogeyman had manifested in the form of a virus and no matter how much they pointed out anyone and everyone could get it, there were still the little digs that stung.

So far it's been contained to small groups. They said it without saying it – so far it's just the addicts and the queers.

Well, Mrs Judgy Judge with the pursed lips and the hideous matching track suit, you can see we're here and you'd best get used to it.

'Sherlock Holmes, come through, please.'

Sherlock locked his eyes on mine.

'Do you want me to come with you?' I reached for his hand but he didn't yet move for mine.

He looked at his shoes, back to me, down to his shoes again. He nodded and took my hand.

'At least one of us needs to be brave.'

1989

'...but you all know what he would have said about all this fuss. He hated parties and said funerals were an illogical waste of time and money...'

John stared down at his lap. When did the skin of his thumbs get so wrinkled? Maybe he should drink more water. He hated water. It was boring. All tasted like blood and sand to him now, anyway. He'd rather drink tea. He could murder a coffee right now. Or that entire bottle of Glenfiddich behind the cornflakes.

He rubbed his eyes with his thumb and forefinger, wondering how many friends he'd lost now to that fucker of a virus. The knot in his gut twisted tighter. He couldn't remember and he hated himself for it.

Sherlock crept his hand across and draped it atop John's, quirking his bottom lip in the way that ever and always asked, *all right?*

John's own lips were pressed tight. He didn't know what would emerge if he opened his mouth. Probably not words.

And when had he started shaking? Or was it Sherlock who was shaking? Sherlock. He was still here. Right here.

He shook his head and squeezed Sherlock's hand. *I'm so very much not all right.*

Sherlock brought John's hand to his chest and there they sat. They'd get through this together, breath by breath.

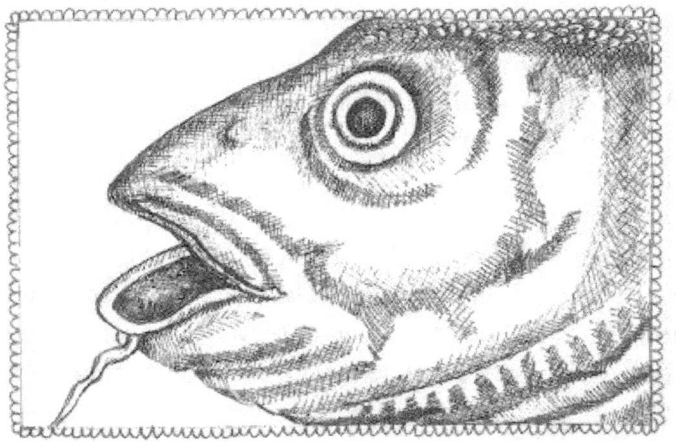

1687

'I won't have this in my house, Mr Watson. Mr Holmes is drunk and I shan't be the one cleaning his vomit off the stairs.'

John waved away the rest of his landlady's complaints. 'I'll see to it, Mrs Hudson.'

He tiptoed up the stairs and set a tentative hand on the doorknob. It was pulled away by a tornado of smoke, silk, and furious man. John was dragged inside by his cravat and the door slammed shut behind him.

'Fffish, John.' Sherlock, stinking of wine, crowded John against the wall. 'That's why they won't ffund my bee compendium. The Royal Society have spent all the fffucking money on a history of ffffish.'

He slid a drunken hand down the side of John's face. 'And now that stargazing tart Halley is gathering coin again, and do you know for what? For that rich bastard Newton's mathematical principles of philosophy of mathematical dullness which he could jolly well pay for his own damn self.' He blew a wet raspberry.

John tried in vain to peel wandering fingers from his neck, his face, his nostrils. 'My love, you're raving.'

'Mathematics! They've stooped to mathematics. Spare me. Next they'll shake out the coffers for a map of the stars.'

He gave a small sob and a hiccough. 'Why don't they like my bees?'

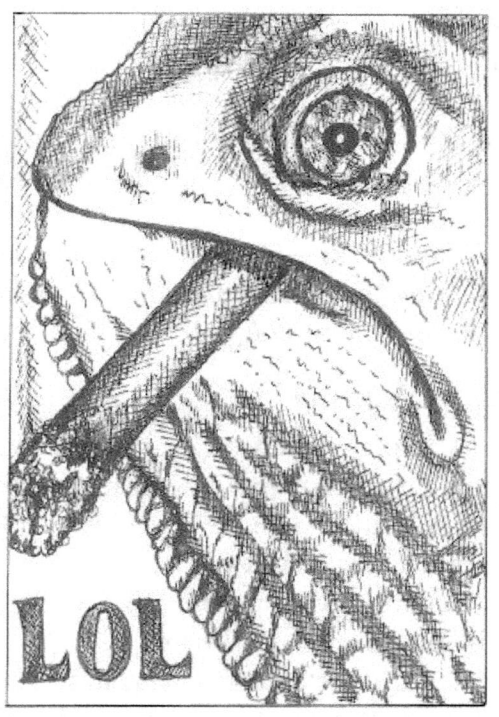

2015

THE FIRST TIME THINGS WENT AWRY SHERLOCK'S LAPTOP FROZE AND disappeared the database he'd been making for several hundred blends of tobacco ash. He spent the night weeping with his head in John's lap. He never saw the pop-up notification with the cigar-smoking cartoon lizard that said *LOL*.

The second time John's phone froze, utterly unresponsive as he tried to call Sherlock while running after Moran. A bullet grazing his ear was enough for John to forget his phone had chimed an 8-bit melody of *Run, Rabbit, Run* instead of dialing.

The third time Sherlock tried to find a signal in the middle of the Channel while his dinghy deflated. The phone clicked through to voice help and said, *'Bon voyage, Mr Holmes.'*

The water-ski rescue John pulled off became legend.

A day later, Mrs Hudson pushed her glasses up and put her ex-MI5 tech knowledge to use on the devices Sherlock dumped on her kitchen table.

'Very clever, adapted to all platforms. You've a virus, dear. Same on all of them, see?' She turned the laptop. 'Moriarty.exe.'

'What can it do?'

Mrs Hudson drew him into the next room and whispered, 'Remote access to camera and microphone for one. I'll clean these up and we'll track it down.' She gave him a wink. 'No one but me bugs my boys.'

1739

'YOU EXPECT THE ROGUE CAME THIS WAY, HOLMES?'

'Undoubtedly, Watson. A skilful enquiry of the fine gentlemen of this establishment and I trust we shall have our man.' Holmes sipped at his coffee.

'Fine gentlemen indeed, seeking their mollies for the night at King's. And by no means an occasion for you to find your fill of this execrable muddy potion? You know well it keeps you up all night.'

'Ha!' Holmes barked. He took Watson's hand, pulled it below the bench and placed it between his legs. 'You complain, sir?'

With his free hand Watson seized Holmes's coffee and swigged the remainder. With the other hand he squeezed.

'I never complain, sir, but I'll drink your gritty concoction and match your hours tonight. Boy!' He called to the tiny angel with his tray and gossamer wings.

As Watson reached out for another two cups, Holmes stood suddenly and leapt over the table crying, 'There's our man, Watson.'

Both cups clattered to the floor, coffee flooding over the bench and Watson's frock coat.

'There's my only silks ruined,' he muttered. 'If a Mr Gregson asks, boy, you did not see us here. And if you're as clever as you look you'll make sure no one else saw us either.' He winked and as he left tossed a shilling to the boy.

1937

'WHAT WAS THAT MONSTROSITY?'

Sherlock took a long draw on his cigarette. 'You're a man of science, John. Tell me, was that half man, half ape the missing link?'

John brought Sherlock's hand and cigarette to his mouth. His hands remained clasped around Sherlock's as he exhaled and took another puff. 'I don't know what to think.'

'You're shaking, dear boy.' Sherlock dropped his cigarette and threaded his fingers through John's.

'That *thing...*'

'Was a fake.'

'What?'

'Clear as day.'

'How can you know?'

With twinkling eyes Sherlock drew his hands down John's chest. 'All this time' – he wrapped arms around his waist and drew him close – 'you still doubt me?'

'Of course not.' John nipped at Sherlock's jaw. 'But do stop nattering and tell me.'

'They're all off exploring the Amazon these days, every man and his pet parrot. Looking for the newest thing to astound the British public. Clearly this lot found nothing but a local girl willing to stick an ape mask on her face and slouch her way to London.'

'She was making expressions.'

'It was a very clever mask, I grant you.'

'But why on earth–?'

'Fame, dear boy. Acclaim. Bring back a sensation from the new world, bask in the money and glory.'

'I damn near soiled myself.'

'Darling, I'm always here to save your britches.'

1595

PART 1

Dearest sir, my husband,

I must, may god give to me the fortitude, inform you and thus satisfy my duty, with all the honour and love i bear you, of a curse that hath befallen us. That our house be troubled by two strange men – gentlemen I shall not call them, for no gentleman ought to break down the door and steal into the house of another, unwelcomed.

Here they arrived one week gone being the 22nd day of October, and show no sign of leaving though we beseech them incessantly.

The taller and madder of the two hath settled in the great hall where he hath assembled all manner of devices being for the observation of ghosts, so said he to his companion.

They hath torn down the tapestries upon which they sleep in unholy embrace, unheeding of mine complaints. And in mine turn about the gardens hath I observed the shorter of the two with a dowsing stick while the other spent an hour knocking on the walls of the buttery, so said cook, though she bade him leave, banging the pots when he gave her no heed.

I pray you come home, sir, and beseech god to bless you and speed you to me, for each day they remain I descend further into madness.

Your faithful wife, Bess

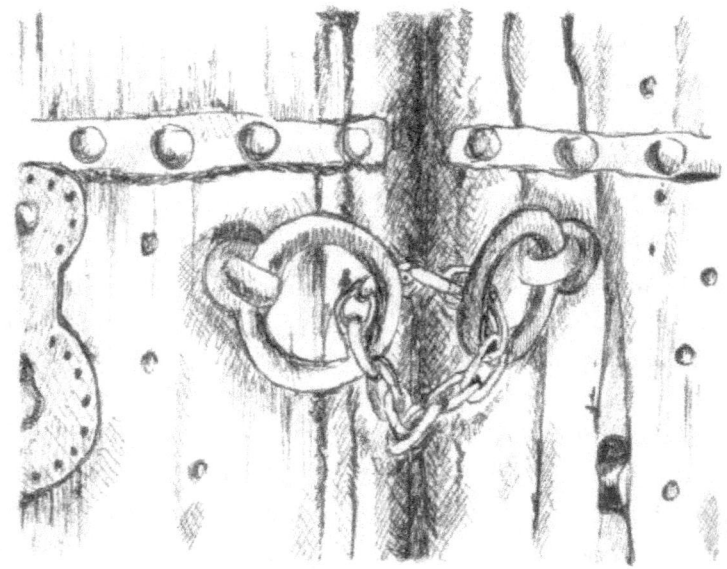

1595

PART 2

'YOU ARE CERTAIN *THIS* IS THE HOUSE, MY LORD?' ASKED WATSON.

Lord Holmes peered up at the ruinous manor looming before them, squinting in the sunlight at crumbling parapets.

'Not as certain as I was, though the coachman seemed to be.'

'And he sped away fast as he could the moment our feet hit the ground. You remember?'

Lord Holmes hummed and rattled the locked chains on the charred wooden door. He turned, shielding his eyes and casting over the expanse of overgrown land they had walked half the morning through.

'This is Heddley Hall, though Sir Beauclair's most fervent letter betting I would find evidence of the existence of spirits here did not mention the state of the manor.'

Watson followed his lord's gaze. 'Are we to shelter here the week? Is there a roof to shelter beneath? Is the structure safe?' He knocked on the door arch.

'Here our work has brought us and here we shall stay, unless there is another residence near where we may beg of their hospitality.'

'None that we passed. And it is hardly work, sir, when your primary conviction is to win a shilling off a man.'

'And it shall be the easiest shilling I shall ever earn, Mr Watson. I've every faith we shall find here not a single wight or bogle.

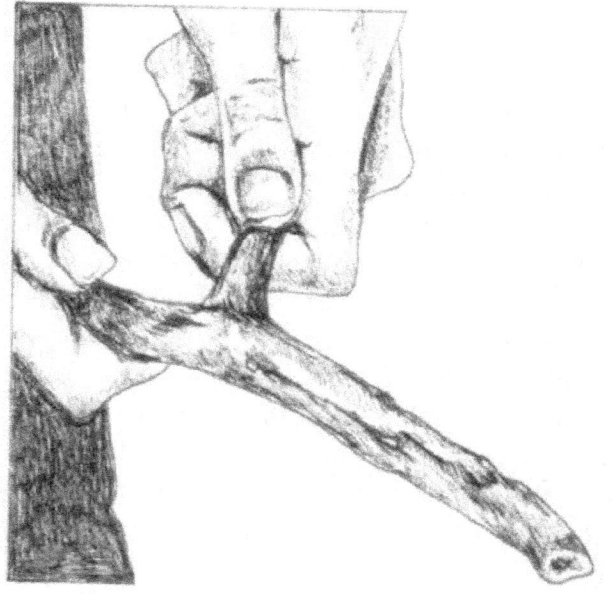

1595

PART 3

OF OUR SPIRIT HUNTING AT HEDDLEY HALL:

The manor is in greater ruin than Sir Beauclair forewarned – my cloak remains damp from the rain.

My lord amazes with his devices. I know not where in his trunk he hid all the instruments he assembled about the hall. Mayhap the trunk is bottomless and he is a sorcerer. I know not.

I wished to make use of myself and being the goodly and trusting master he is, Lord Holmes gave to me a dowsing stick with which to seek disturbances in the stables.

Upon my return, having found nought but mud and rotten boards, my lord – impressed with the manner in which I handled the dowsing stick – prayed I handle *his* stick. A merry divergence was had, though my knees gave no thanks to the flagstones.

Sir Beauclair told us of the Lady Elizabeth, a spirit who haunted him as a child. I will swear to it I heard a clamour of pots being struck in the kitchens during the day, and whispered voices when all was still in the night, though my lord swears he did not, and more besides we neither of us saw a thing.

Though the manor gave me an ill boding, I trust my lord's wisdom and declare him a shilling richer and winner of the bet.

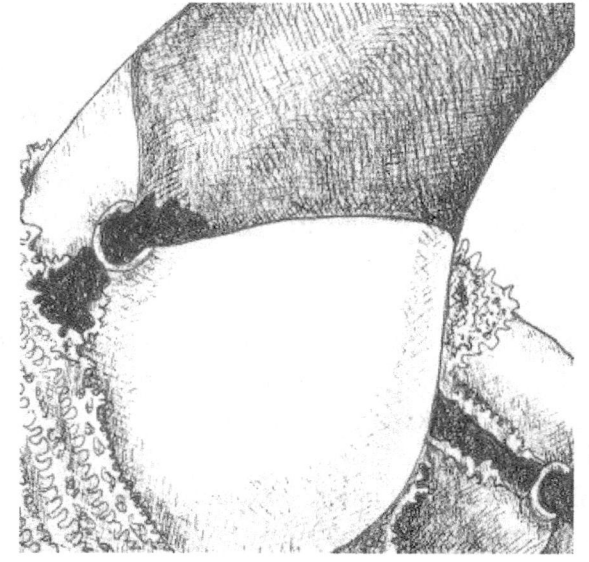

1931

SHERLOCK PROWLED THE DANCE FLOOR EDGE. HEAT AND SMOKE AND SWEAT hung like fog. Bodies heaved and bumped, bounced and twirled to the dizzy jazz.

Across the room Johanna sat on Herr Bauerfeind's lap, legs swinging. Herr Metzger leaned across their small table and drew on his cigar. With a leer he blew smoke across Johanna's face.

Sherlock gritted her teeth and thumbed her pistol as she watched Bauerfeind's hand slip higher up Johanna's dress. She sashayed closer, passing Tangoing Pox Trotters. If this worked, a substantial but discreet thank you from His Majesty and Prime Minister MacDonald awaited them back home.

Johanna fiddled with her pearls. Her laugh tinkled above the music as she threw her head back to see Sherlock weaving around tables behind them. She ran her nails in a light dance down Bauerfeind's cheek. A hard tug on her pearls sent them on a cascade and bouncing beneath dancing feet. In mock surprise Johanna leapt up, knocking the table and sending a stein of beer over Metzger.

As chaos descended on the dancehall, Sherlock slipped behind them. She swapped Metzger's briefcase with a duplicate, and slipped away.

Three minutes later in the drizzly alley outside the Schubert-Saal, Johanna hooked her arm through Sherlock's and pressed a lingering kiss to her lips. 'Let's say goodbye to Berlin.'

1603

I STARTLED AWAKE, THINKING FOR A TIME THE END HAD COME. BUT I KNEW those hands, on my shoulder, on my cheek. And the hushed voice urging me awake. The Protestant pursuivants – scouring the country for priests such as I – even now were on their way.

He caught me as I leapt up with a cry, held me close and murmured, 'Peace, peace.'

We had prepared for this moment, yet by the meagre light of the moon I saw the glint of tears.

Hand in hand we descended to the kitchen, and in the darkness found the great chimney. For below the house, with skill beyond compare, my love had built what would be my salvation.

'Hurry, John,' Lord Sherlock thrust a sack of provisions, enough for a great many days, into my hands and drew me to a burning kiss. 'And silence, yes? Until I come for you.'

I hesitated, 'My lord, if they should find…' I began.

He silenced me with another kiss and a firm, 'No,' then pushed me into the hearth wherein I ducked beneath the lintel and reached up to open a cleverly masked door.

I clambered up. Before sealing my priest hole, I called out below, 'You won't forget me?'

My lord's low honeyed laugh rang out. 'Never, my love. Now up into your byre.'

1100

BROTHER SHERLOCK STARED AT THE BODY OF THE KING. HE'D BEEN STARING in silence too long.

'What shall we say?' Brother John whispered.

They glanced over their shoulders at the glaring lords gathered in the transept.

'What are *they* saying?' Sherlock tilted his head back.

'Henry is to be king. He demanded they open the treasury, and is away to London for the crown.'

Sherlock grunted. 'So the king, his brother, and the best archer in the land go hunting in the forest.'

'Is this the start of a joke?' John asked.

'The king's body is abandoned in the forest with an arrow to the heart, the archer is disappeared, and the king's brother runs to Winchester to seize the treasury and the crown. It's hardly a mystery.'

'Yes, but we can't accuse the king of killing the king in order to be king. What are we going to *say?*'

'I'm as happily attached to my head as you, John, and would prefer to keep it that way.'

'Call it an accident?'

'Good idea. Tragic death, wayward arrow, god's judgement on his deplorable reign, et cetera. And throw something portentous in. Perhaps blood boiling out of the ground.'

'Bit dramatic.'

'It won't raise an eyebrow, John. Now, if we were talking nonsense like men flying to the moon or talking books...'

1977

ANY OTHER TIME THE SOUND OF DESPERATE FEET AND THE THUNDERING OF their hearts would have been the only sounds spurring Sherlock and John in a chase. Now they could hear nothing above the roar of a thousand flaming torches and the riot of singing that was Up Helly Aa.

They raced through the thronging streets of Lerwick, toward the wooden galley. The only evidence that could convict their suspect was about to be incinerated in a bonfire there, to farewell winter and welcome the light.

They saw the dragon prow just as the Guizer Jarl called a *hip hip* to celebrate the galley builders. Sparks rained from torches as madly costumed torchbearers circled closer to the ship.

Sherlock and John shoved through the condensing crowd of tourists and townsfolk closing in around them.

As a *hip hip* for the Jarl arose, Sherlock pushed past men dressed as Vikings, flying nuns, and a gang of Flintstones and Rubbles. The galley was right there.

John grabbed Sherlock's arm as a *hooray* for Up Helly Aa roared out. They were too late.

The first of the torches flew into the galley, then the next and the next until the ship was a flaming porcupine of torch handles.

John held his arms tight around a struggling Sherlock. Some cases were not meant to be.

190 BCE

PART 1

THE SACRED WAY THRONGED WITH PETITIONERS AS MYCROPHTIS PUFFED UP the incline. His nose wrinkled against the bright sun, at the human traffic around him, everyone urged onward by the column of smoke rising from the sacrifices.

The Oracle was open for business.

'You.' Mycrophtis untied his purse and threw it to his proxy. 'I'm to be given priority.' He noted the slight roll in the young man's eyes. He'd reflect the insolence in his payment, he could be sure of that. He watched the young man run up ahead, admiring the boy's dark muscled thighs and bemoaning his own weak limbs.

Sweat beaded on his brow, a moist heaven for the flies. He resisted the urge to swat them with the laurel he clasped in his clammy hands. This heat was intolerable. The rituals, the questioning of the priests had set his head spinning. All he wanted was his bed, some good meat, and an entire bottle of wine. Perhaps this boy could be persuaded to join him, for the right price.

At the temple the proxy returned to lead him past the lesser supplicants to the door. 'Mycrophtis of Orchomenus,' the boy announced.

Mycrophtis's eyes drifted up to the words above the threshold before stepping into the smoky gloom. *Nothing In Excess*. His hand involuntarily settled on his belly.

190 BCE

PART 2

THE SULPHUROUS AIR HAD HIS EYES WATERING AND HIS THROAT CONSPIRING to put an end to this breathing business. Mycrophtis gathered himself, wiped away his sweat and tears, the rivulets from his nose. He'd built a treasury outside to rival Athens' – he ought to remain dignified.

At a nod from the priests, he stepped toward the curtain. It breathed in waves, in and out as the earthy vapours tendrilled beneath it. Mycrophtis wondered if he was imagining the shadows writhing. He raised his chin and cleared his throat.

'My sister Seralocia's Spartan lover, Iohanna, she encourages my sister's wayward behaviour. I wish to know if I should have her dealt with, for my sister's sake?'

A shriek pierced the air.

Mycrophtis jumped.

A hoarse snake-like hiss began a babble of gibberish. *Run, laugh, fight, love?* Mycrophtis tried to find meaning in the noise. When the words petered out in a whine the priests huddled to consult.

'Your sister and her lover are stronger together than apart,' they harmonised.

'She told me to run.'

'She was not speaking to you.'

Mycrophtis pursed his lips. His status held no sway here, only his money. Better together, then. He supposed he must heed the words of Apollo, no matter his disapproval or fear. He sighed. Being a big brother was a tricky business.

1940

My Dearest John, Captain

Lest you hear the dreadful news of how near this Blitz (as the newsmen are calling it) came to us and fear the worst, let me assure you all is well. 221B still stands and misses you dearly. As do we all.

Now to the news of the tragic deaths in Marble Arch and our narrow escape.

I'd returned from meeting with my brother, who sends his greetings and gave me a fine 55-year-old Mortlach to be opened on your return.

Mrs Hudson insisted we look in on a Mr Chapman on Seymour St. Our Hudson is sweet on the fellow and is making her move. Ask me how I know in your reply.

As we left, the sirens whirred their haunted song. One wonders when this nightly dirge will end – the blasted things are incessant, as is Jerry.

Thankfully, we did not traipse down the nearby underground, going home first for our blankets and Sukey (Mrs Hudson's new kitten) and joined the crowd at Marylebone instead. I owe my life to a cat, John. It is absurd.

Return to me soon.

Yours,

Sherlock

P.S. Mrs Hudson implored me to send regards and butter biscuits. The regards I send gladly, the butter biscuits I've eaten. You and your crop can tell me just how naughty I've been.

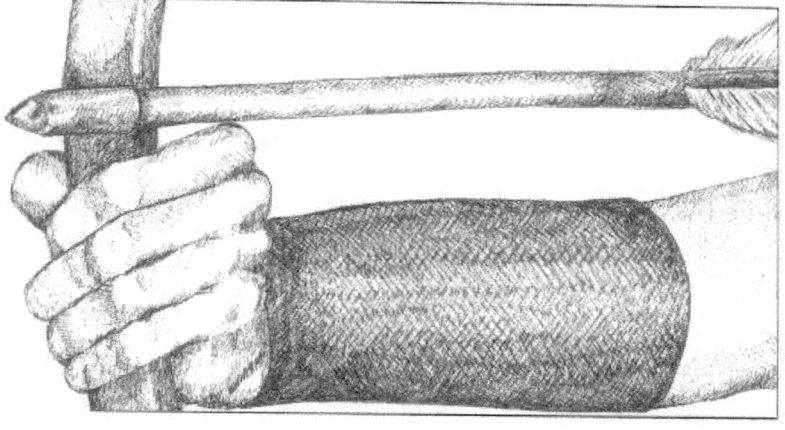

1211

Upon the greenwood road came wandering
Two fellows on horseback merry with song
They happened upon a man of the green
And saw in his eyes he would do them a wrong
Well met, my good men, how do you this day?
Said that vile villain Robyn the Hoode
Blessed we be, John said, drawing his dagger
But for you it bodes ill and not good
Down from their steeds came Sherlock and John
An arrow Robyn nocked in his bow
But before he could strike the heart of his love
Sherlock leapt, knocking Robyn down low
To the sheriff forthwith and into a cell
Robyn Hoode they did heckle and shackle
Your villainous days are over, good sir
Arm-in-arm they waved off with a cackle
In the greenwood again they met with a gang
Of green men a-snarl and a-scowling
Sherlock looked to his John, John shot him a wink
And with arms drawn, leapt in a-growling
Said Robyn Hoode's man, the beast John Little
Peace now, we serve Coeur de Lion
Sherlock laughed merrily, that Frenchman be-damned
For England we fight not kings absent so long
With a bolt to the heart, Sherlock shot Little John
And with sword John had them herded like cattle
The skirmish now ended, blood flowing a-stream
Side-by-side John and Sherlock won the battle.

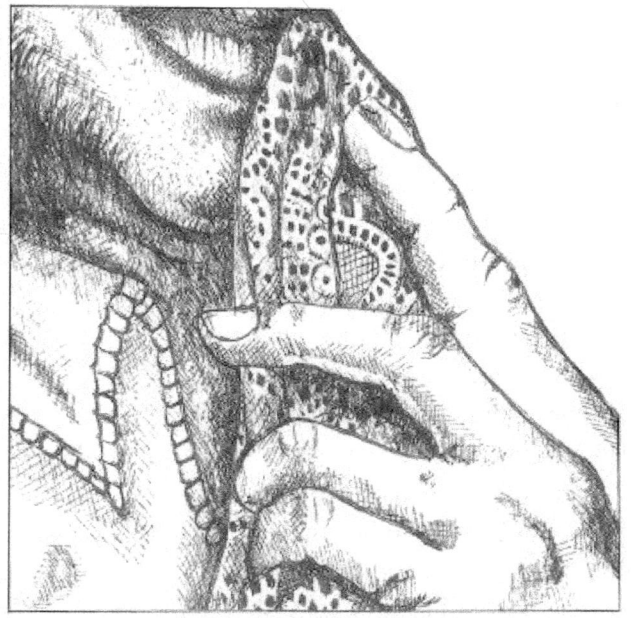

1710

'YOU TWO! I'VE TOLD YOU, STOP SNEAKING ABOUT. YOU'RE FRIGHTENING me customers away, they knows who you is. Out of me house afore I–'

'Miss Do-ho-hoddle!' Mister Watson stretched her name to four syllables, smacked the back of his head on the mantle, and spurted his release deep down Mister Holmes's throat, all while maintaining a disarming smile.

Unlike Mister Holmes, who pulled off with an obscene slurp and wiped the corners of his mouth with a dainty lace handkerchief. *He* scowled a storm at Miss Doddle, flushing a deep red down his chest.

'I shall set my boys on you.'

'Truly?' Mister Holmes rose, towering over the tiny woman. 'I could topple your empire and every other molly house with it, madam. Or cooperate and I shall ensure your good name remains so. 'Tis your choice.'

A beat of silence broke with Miss Doddle wringing her hands and dripping a saccharine smile. 'May I assist you gentlemen in some case or other this day?'

Mister Holmes pulled a letter from his frock coat. 'You may. The whereabouts of every name on this list, a bottle of your best Malmsey, and a pot of clean oil – for our privities. Oh, and a moment in your marrying room,' – Mister Holmes caught Mister Watson's hand and brought it to his lips–' for a blessing.'

19,873 BCE

THE ONE CALLED OCK TOOK THE HAND OF THE ONE CALLED HON AND LAID it against the wall of rock, letting go with a little pat that said, *stay there*. Before Ock had slurped up his mix of ochre, Hon had dropped his hand in disinterest.

'Home we go.' Hon waved a hand toward the dimming light at the cave mouth. 'Sun to sleep.'

Ock placed Hon's hand back on the rock, holding him by the wrist. He knee-crawled close and blew a spray of the red ochre over Hon's hand and the rock. Hon peeled his hand away, leaving his print stencilled in the deep earthy red.

'We home go, much time I you touch.' Ock nuzzled behind Hon's ear and grunted soft and low. He placed his own hand next to the fresh print and pointed at the bowl he had mixed the yellow ochre in. He nudged Hon with his sharp long nose.

Hon did as he was bid. He slurped up the ochre mix and held it in his mouth, looking like a pufferfish. He waddled closer and spat out a spray onto Ock's hand and the rock, leaving a yellow hand stencilled next Hon's own.

Side by side they admired their art; the ghosts of their fingertips touching on the rock and the sun setting behind.

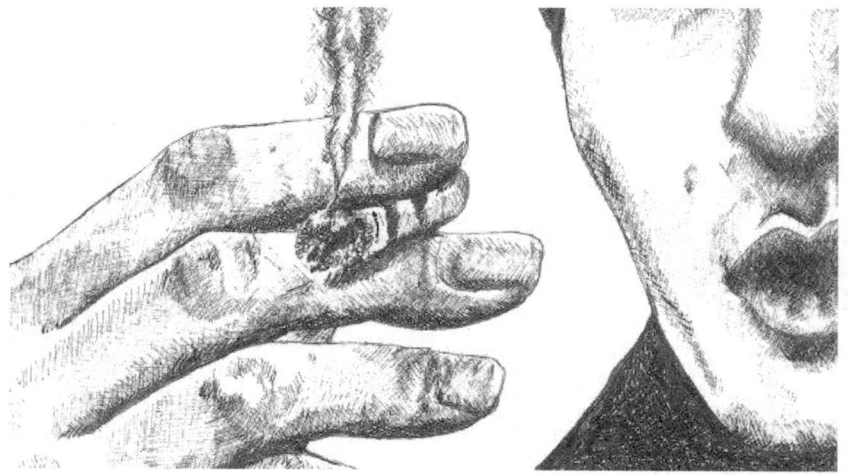

1980

IAN CURTIS'S MOODY VOCALS DRIFTED ALONG THE ALLEYWAY, A GRIMY thoroughfare of broken bottles and cigarette butts between student housing.

'Nice area, mate.' John dripped sarcasm onto his boots.

'Why?' Stamford called back over his shoulder. 'You looking for the Ritz?'

John shrugged. 'Fair dues. I'll take what I can get.'

Stamford gestured him on. 'Good. This guy's been looking for a flatmate for months. You'll see why. Thought you might get along.'

Emerging from the alley, they turned into the house on the left. The bright blue door was open, Joy Division's *Atmosphere* vibrating the walls.

'Upstairs,' Stamford shouted.

At the landing he rapped on the door and entered. Silhouetted against the window was a reedy man playing a jaunty harmony on his violin to the dismal music downstairs, three lit cigarettes in his mouth.

Without missing a beat he turned sharp dark eyes to his visitors. He threw the violin on the sofa and wended through piles of books towards them. He took one cigarette out of his mouth and popped it into Stamford's with his eyes glued to John's.

'You smoke?'

'No.'

'Good. Nasty, filthy habit.' He took the cigarette out of Stamford's mouth.

'Hope you don't mind mess.'

'S'fine.'

'I'm a moody bastard.'

'Me too.'

Sherlock shrugged. 'I play violin quite badly.'

'Don't mind.'

Sherlock smiled. 'Brilliant.'

2019

Part 1

'That's a lovely piece. Are you a composer yourself?'

John was addressing an arse. It was a nice arse. A fine arse. So he was happy to address it while the busker put away his violin.

'That sounded like I'm a composer too. Or something. I'm not. I mean, I don't know anything about classical music. I mean, I know a few pieces I like but I couldn't name any composers or anything. Ha.'

He scratched the back of his neck. *Stop being an arse, John. Stop thinking about arse. Jesus! Stop talking.*

The busker clipped his case closed, turned, and jolted back when he noticed John standing right in front of him. He gave him a questioning look.

'Sorry, I'm a babbler. Sometimes. I mean, I babble when I'm nervous. I don't know why I'd be nervous. I just wanted to say I enjoyed you. *Listening* to you. And your body. Moving. When you play. Watching you *move* when you *play.*'

Jesus, John, walk away, walk away now. His feet refused, staying rooted right there in front of his embarrassment.

He waved a frantic hand at the still-open case of CDs. 'Are you selling those? Are you Sherlock? Of course you are! It says right there. Fuck. I...need to stop talking.'

John shoved a thumb in his mouth and *bit.*

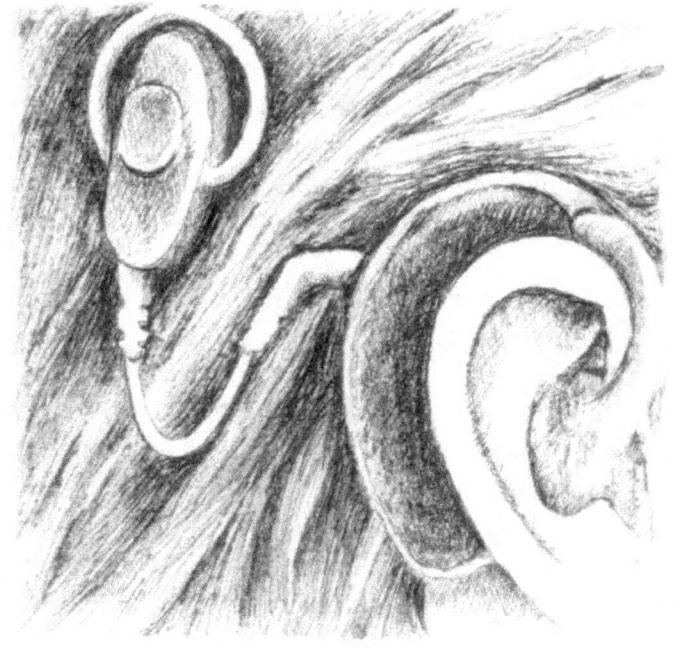

2019

PART 2

THE BUSKER GRINNED, THEN SIGNED AND SPOKE IN A GENTLE MUTED ACCENT. 'Yes, I'm a composer, yes, I'm Sherlock, and yes, I am selling CDs.'

At last in control of his babbling, John said nothing.

'Sorry I didn't hear you. I like to feel my music, so I turn this off when I play.' Sherlock reached for the sleek black speech processor behind his ear. He pulled the small magnet off his head and fiddled with it as he asked, 'Was there something else you wanted?'

It took John a moment to finish chewing on his nail. 'Uh. Oh. Um. M-maybe I could buy you a drink? And you could let me feel your music? I mean – I didn't mean… Oh, hell.'

Throwing his head back and laughing in wheezy barks, Sherlock signed rapidly with his elegant hands. John blinked his lack of comprehension.

'I said, lucky for you I didn't hear you say that out loud.'

Sherlock tucked the processor back behind his ear, his gaze suddenly caught by a passerby in a black hoodie. He bent to hastily pack up his CDs.

'But maybe you can repeat it. I can't promise I won't laugh again, but my answer will be yes, please.'

Sherlock handed John the box of CDs.

'In the meantime, how do you feel about chasing a burglar?'

A Bit More Story About the Stories in

A Question of Time

2017   THE HIVE AT KEW GARDENS

The Hive is a sculpture located in the Royal Botanic Gardens in Kew. It is a 17-metre tall aluminium honeycomb beehive designed by artist Wolfgang Buttress, but it's not just a static object to be looked at. It's an interactive conduit between the visitor and a real beehive.

Inside The Hive, 1000 LED lights twinkle on and off. These aren't a random assortment of party lights, they're driven by the activity of real bees in a real hive whose movements are picked up by vibration sensors to be interpreted inside the sculpture by the lights.

The activity in the real beehive is also represented inside the sculpture by a soundscape consisting of pre-recorded sounds, recorded by musicians interpreting the sounds of a working beehive.

1816   NAPOLEON 'OLD BONEY' BONAPARTE

Old Boney was a British nickname for Napoléon Bonaparte, statesman, military leader, and emperor of the French from 1804 to 1814.

While England was at war with the French, fear of invasion was very real, and Napoléon was used as a sort of bogeyman for naughty children, seen explicitly in the nursery rhyme *Naughty Baby* as a cannibalistic force to be feared by unruly whippersnappers.

> Baby, baby, naughty baby
> Hush, you squalling thing I say
> Peace this moment, peace, or maybe
> Bonaparte will pass this way

1086 THE DOMESDAY BOOK

Twenty years (or possibly 19) after the Battle of Hastings, William the Conqueror ordered a thorough survey of his new realm, England. To determine the worth of every manor in the land (and therefore how much sweet, sweet tax he could demand), his officials asked a specific set of questions of the local reeve and a number of representative peasants.

These questions included how many ploughs and mills the manor owned, how much woodland, how much pasture, how many freemen, villagers, slaves, and a good account of how much each manor was owed by each freeman. It was a remarkable feat, carried out in less than a year, and collected into what was known as the Domesday Book (pronounced /ˈduˈmzdejˈ/).

Despite the way it sounds, the 'Dome' in Domesday is, and at the same time isn't, the 'doom' as we know it today, but a word more akin to judgement, ordinance, and law.

1666 THE GREAT FIRE OF LONDON

For four days in 1666, from September 2nd to the 5th, London was aflame. It began after midnight in Pudding Lane in a baker's shop owned by Thomas Farynor, quite possibly caused by a rogue ember from an oven. It *almost* certainly wasn't Sherlock Holmes, but we can't know for sure.

After a long dry summer, the mainly wooden constructions of the city, packed together with their pitched and thatched rooves, were a ready tinder for the conflagration.

About 80% of the city was destroyed, including St Paul's Cathedral and over 13000 houses. This destruction led to the city being rebuilt on a grand scale using better, durable, slightly less flammable building materials. It also led to an organised fire service and the beginnings of the insurance industry.

As 1665 was the last significant outbreak of the plague, killing 80,000 Londoners, the Great Fire was also said to have cleansed the city of all the rats and fleas said to have carried the disease.

Accounts of the time include that of diarist Samuel Pepys, who mentioned even the king, Charles II, was seen helping fight the flames.

1962   THE BIG FREEZE

The winter of 1962-63 was one of the coldest winters ever recorded in Britain, with January of 1963 having an average temperature of -2.1°C (28.2°F). The technical term for this is Flipping Cold.

At the time the story is set, northerly winds from a high pressure system near Iceland began to move in, bringing with it heavy snowfall on Boxing Day. After that, the cold seemed there to stay, with some areas of the country having snow cover lasting 2 months.

Let's hope Mrs Hudson agreed to that central heating.

1703   THE GREAT STORM

In 1703 southern England was hit by hurricane-force winds that still count as one of the worst storms that has ever hit Britain.

We know so much about this storm thanks mostly to Daniel Defoe, who collected first-hand accounts from around the country, but also from reports of the amount of structural damage it caused.

An estimated 8000 to 15000 people were killed as well as many animals, thousands of trees were uprooted, and ships were blown from their moorings.

Close to 2000 chimney stacks collapsed, just like the one in the story, and as the wind picked up once people were abed, many were killed by their chimneys as they slept.

1348   The Black Death

The Black Death was a pandemic that swept through Asia and into Europe between the years 1347 and 1351, killing an estimated one-third of Europe's population. This varied from area to area, with some areas losing from one-eighth to two-thirds of their population. In England, near 1000 villages were completely wiped out.

It is widely accepted that The Black Death was caused by the plague, which is a bacterial disease caused by *Yersinia pestis.* However, there is also some evidence that it may have been caused by a viral disease.

Whatever the cause of the disease, the wide-scale disaster left a much changed society. Death became a preoccupation in art, anti-Semitism rose as blame was placed on the Jewish population, and the loss of much of the labour force left many landholders ruined or forced them to provide wages and better living terms.

1731   Ashburnham House Fire

On October 23rd 1731, the unfortunately (aptly) named Ashburnham House in Westminster suffered a devastating fire. Inside was Sir Robert Cotton's library – moved there, ironically, for safety – which contained the greatest collection of Anglo-Saxon manuscripts in the country, packed onto 14 bookshelves, each overseen by a bust of a Roman Emperor.

Thanks to the swift and brave actions of the trustees who carted manuscripts away or threw them from the windows, only 13 of almost 1000 manuscripts were lost completely, though hundreds were damaged terribly by either the fire or the water used to put it out.

One of those saved manuscripts was *Cotton Vitellius A xv.* (the

15th volume on the first shelf under the bust of emperor Vitellius) AKA the Nowell Codex, AKA the Beowulf manuscript – one of the oldest examples of written Old English literature. And thank goodness for that, otherwise we'd have been robbed of this most glorious of opening lines:

Hwæt we gardena	*in geardagum*
Listen! We Spear Danes	in days gone by
þeodcyninga	*þrym gefrunon*
of those kings of the people	we have heard of their glory.
hu ða æþelingas	*ellen fremedon*
How those noblemen	did brave things.

1687 THE PRINCIPIA

Sir Isaac Newton's *Philosophiae Naturalis Principia Mathematica*, or The Principia to its mates, was an eventual trilogy that gave us such gems as the Laws of Motion and the theory of gravity. However, it had a bit of a tough time getting published.

The Royal Society had just spent its entire book budget on publishing *The History of Fish* by Francis Willughby. Sadly for old Franky-boy and the Royal Society's coffers, it was as far from a wild success as a book could be.

No wonder poor Sherlock threw a wobbly.

Luckily for Newton (who was super rich, by the way, the cheeky sod could have funded his own book) his buddy Edmond Halley of comet fame (who was also super rich) coughed up the funds for The Principia himself.

1937 THE APE-MAN

This story is fabricated but came about due to the sensational photographs of a mysterious ape-man found in the Brazilian jungle – or so it was reported in a Dutch magazine in the 1930s. These photos swept the internet in 2012 and caused much debate as to the origin of the ape man.

They show a hunched man with a deeply furrowed brow and enlarged lips and nose. The ape man's authenticity has been debated, though for most it is clear that some rudimentary prosthetic make-up was used to create an approximation of ape-like features.

For what purpose this was done is unknown but, as Sherlock claims, it was most likely for the thrill of the spotlight and 15 minutes of fame.

The things that didn't make it... aka the outtakes

1948 THE SOMERTON MAN

One of the most intriguing cases for international murder mystery buffs is the Tamam Shud case or the strange story of the Somerton Man – named after Somerton Beach near Adelaide, South Australia, where his body was found lying with legs outstretched on the sand and his head propped up against the seawall.

No official cause of death was found, though poison or asphyxiation were possibilities, and no positive identification was made despite international distribution of his photograph and fingerprints.

His build was athletic with unusually pronounced calves, like those of a dancer or runner. All identifying tags had been removed from his clothing, but among his few possessions were found items intimating he may have arrived from the U.S.

That this occurred during the Cold War made the theory that he was a spy an attractive story.

The Somerton Man is also known as the Tamam Shud case for the scrap of paper found in his pocket with the words Tamam Shud printed on it. The small rolled-up paper was torn from a copy of a book called the *Rubaiyat of Omar Khayyam*. They are the final words in the book, meaning 'ended' or 'finished'.

The particular book this paper had been torn from was eventually found, having been randomly thrown into the open window of a parked car. This succeeded only in adding more to the mystery. The book was a rare edition and analysis of the final pages revealed the indentation of five written lines of what is assumed to be a code. A code which, to this day, has not been solved.

Amateur and professional sleuths have been investigating this case since 1948, with little success, but hopes lie in eventually having the body exhumed for DNA identification.

The case has so many facets, is so convoluted and mysterious and intriguing it would be impossible to do it justice in 221 words. The beautiful illustration is a detail of a cover of one of the many editions of the *Rubaiyat of Omar Khayyam*.

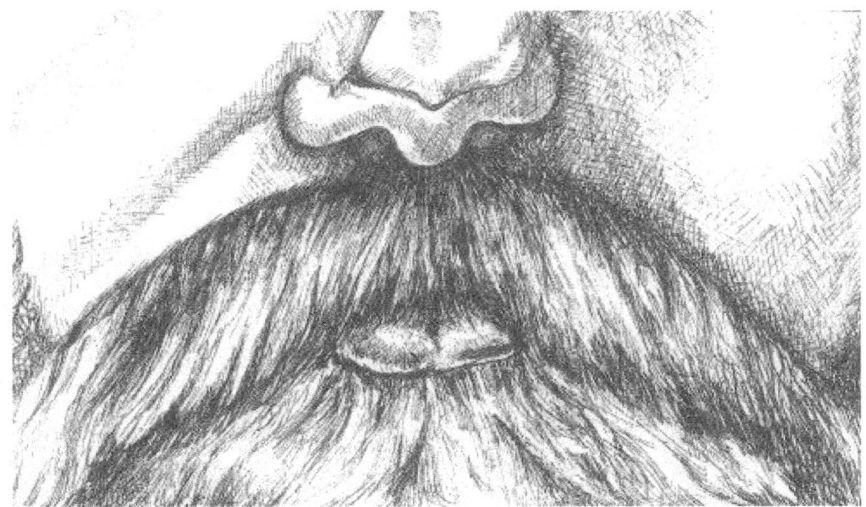

1599 Tycho Brahe

Tycho Brahe was a Danish astronomer from a noble family. His is another story too complicated and interesting to be squeezed into 221 or even 442 words and so didn't find its home among the finished tales.

The first spectacular drawing is of Brahe's impressive facial hair and a hint at his prosthetic nose. During a duel in the dark with his third cousin, he lost the bridge of his nose and for the rest of his life wore a replacement held on with paste or glue. It was said to be gold or silver but after exhumation for analysis in the 20th century, it was found likely to have been made of brass.

The second drawing is a detail from Brahe's own notebook. On this particular page, he noted his observations of the comet seen in 1577.

1381 THE PEASANTS' REVOLT

During the Peasants' Revolt at least 100,000 rebellious peasants led by Wat Tyler marched to London to demand the abolition of serfdom and protest excessive taxation. A rather dry subject to talk about in 221 words. Far more interesting is that the Tower of London was stormed by the rebels because the king, Richard II, had left to meet with the rebel leaders and no one had pulled up the drawbridge. Nice one, fellas.

Unfortunately for the Archbishop of Canterbury, Simon Sudbury, and the Lord High Treasurer, Robert Hales, this meant capture and their heads displayed on pikes on London Bridge. Henry Bolingbroke, the king's young cousin, and later Henry IV, was hiding in a cupboard in the tower and escaped with his life.

The unused drawing is a detail of a 16th century portrait of Henry IV, King of England, all grown up and definitely not hiding in a cupboard.

An interview with the illustrator

Janet Anderton

How did you research the story's various time periods, and develop a style to draw in?

Jamie sent small batches of five stories at a go. It was quite exciting to never know what time period I'd be working on next!

I made a decision at the beginning of the project that I wouldn't draw Holmes and Watson *on* their adventures, as in the original ACD books. Even though I have a very clear idea about who *my* Sherlock and John are, I didn't want to influence the reader. I wanted them to visualise their own version of the pair. So the only way I can describe it is that from the very start I knew I would read each story and 'see' what the story told me to draw.

For example, the one set in the big freeze of 1962. I immediately saw John shucking his boots when he returned home. What boots would John Watson of that period wear? I started researching clothing and found – bingo! – Chelsea boots.

What would John's boots look like? They'd be well kept, he looks after them, he's an army man. He spends a lot of time on his feet, he wouldn't wear cheap shoes. Then I worked from style books and images on the internet to draw *my* John Watson's boots. I pretty much approached every story like that.

Which two drawings were the trickiest in that regard?

Funnily enough the stories set in modern time. There's almost too much information. Since smart phones have a decent camera, everyone is posting photos on the web. The hardest was the story set in 2017 featuring the Hive, the structure is so complicated that I struggled to draw anything that made any sense. I tried a close up of the struts, but it could have been any metal structure. Finally, the editor suggested drawing bees! Genius!

Another drawing I struggled with was the one from 1937, the monkey mask. Jamie sent me a link to an original news report of a couple scamming the public and the photo in the article gave me the heebie jeebies! I had to close the article, shut down my computer, drive 25 miles and bury it in a field. Nasty picture! Thanks Jamie!

Which is your favourite time period to have drawn for and why?

Really?! Just one? Not going to happen!

I loved drawing the Georgian coffeehouse picture, 1739, because of the patterning on the fabric and the cheeky under the table grope!

I loved the cave painting from 19,873 BCE, the simplicity, the fingers touching.

I loved the 1969 moon landing because the story is so pretty.

I think that's the problem in choosing one particular time period, Jamie's words always made such lovely images spring into my mind.

I really enjoyed every time a little cache of stories popped into my inbox because I knew it would set me off on a tiny time travel adventure, researching time periods I had little or no knowledge of.

Anyhow, if you insist on making me choose, I think it would be 2085, because I adore the story so much, and it's not happened yet has it!

The Author & the Illustrator

JAMIE ASHBIRD

Jamie is a polymath (because she likes that word) and a writer (because she says so) who haunts Melbourne and its northern surrounds. She had her very first published story, a 221B, included in the Improbable Press anthology *A Murmuring of Bees*.

You can find her checking under mushrooms for fairies, coveting moss, staring at sky kittens (clouds), squinching her eyes shut as she walks past a book shop, adding more projects to her pile of craft ideas, learning Norwegian for when she retires there as a small troll in the woods, and doing her gosh-darn best not to eat ice-cream.

JANET ANDERTON

Janet has *finally* accepted that she is an Artist (with a big A), it is a huge relief to herself and to those around her. This is the second book that she has illustrated. The first, *Donald Trunk*, written by Juliet Coombe, is a children's picture book all about Sri Lanka's swimming elephant. Janet also had a story included in the Improbable Press anthology *A Murmuring of Bees*.

Born and raised in the North West of England, Janet is now exiled in the East Midlands, where she is raising a cactus called Spiny Norman, naming upcycled furniture after her friends, and making art.

You can find her on Instagram: janet_makes_art, and Twitter: @SartJanet

Acknowledgements

JAMIE ASHBIRD

Millions of starry-eyed thank yous to Wendy and Narrelle who asked the simple question, would you like to write a book?

To which I replied, um, yeah alright.

And who then said, it'll be illustrated by Janet Anderton.

To which I replied, where's my solid gold fountain pen? Sign me the hell up.

I couldn't have done this without your constant encouragement and support. This entire book is covered in pixie dust.

And to *the* Janet Anderton, who, well, hopefully if you're reading this you've seen what she's gone and done with many a deft stroke of her talented hands. The stories are the illustrations and the illustrations are the stories – it's as simple as that. I couldn't have asked for a better co-creator to try to live up to.

To the Quilldrivers, thank you for putting up with me barely ever writing.

Thanks to my family and friends who did not know I was writing a book of Sherlockian romance. Surprise!

Finally, thank you to all the authors, artists, comedians, musicians, scientists, too many to list but who have all shaped this greyish-pink lump of fatty neurons that sits inside my skull.

JANET ANDERTON

Thank you to Jamie Ashbird for your words. It's been an absolute joy being the other mam to this baby. You are an inspiration, a fellow stationery addict, and a much loved member of my pixie tribe.

A huge smash of the kudos button to Wendy and Narrelle who sparked the idea of us working together. Thank you for all your love, enthusiasm, and patience. Pixie's Assemble!

Love to the founder members of The Tuck and Pop Club and to Molly, my heart on the outside.

To all the strong women who have helped forge me. When women support each other, incredible things happen.

Also from Improbable Press

 AN IMPRINT OF CLAN DESTINE PRESS AUSTRALIA

www.improbablepress.co.uk

THE CASE OF THE MISPLACED MODELS
BY TESSA BARDING

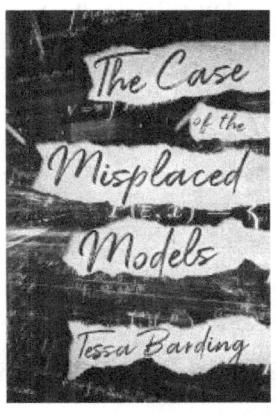

Dr Watson arrives at his surgery one morning to find a stranger about to staple his own leg injury together. Days later, John Watson coincidentally accepts a flatshare with the same man; and before long is laughing, running, and falling in love with the endlessly-fascinating Sherlock Holmes.

While the 'consulting detective' barely seems to notice John, he does agree to help when they learn of the sudden and curious death of John's friend Karim Halabi.

Karim was acidentally shot during a game of laser tag. Case closed, say the police. But as John and Sherlock dig deeper it seems that Karim's death was no accident. It also becomes clear to John that Sherlock's feelings for him are much deeper too.

A STUDY IN VELVET AND LEATHER
BY K. CAINE

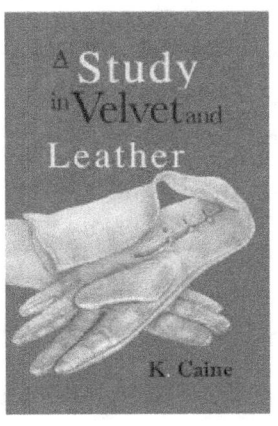

Sharing a flat with Sherlock Holmes should not have posed a problem for John Watson – after all, Watson is gay, Holmes is a woman, and the arrangement is financially convenient.

But when Holmes takes on a complex case involving Irene Adler and a scandalous photograph, she turns to Watson for assistance.

The case leads them everywhere from the opera to a secret Victorian BDSM club, and Watson soon finds himself questioning his partnership with Holmes, his sexuality, and his understanding of himself.

A DREAM TO BUILD A KISS ON
BY NARRELLE M HARRIS

John Watson, invalided army doctor and sometimes artist, and Sherlock Holmes, consulting detective, become flatmates and friends in contemporary London.

Love grows too, despite past betrayals and present dangers – for where you have Holmes and Watson, there too are Moriarty and Moran.

A Dream to Build a Kiss On explores love and family, trust and betrayal, brothers and brothers-in-arms, and forgiveness and revenge.

It's an ongoing tale, told in chapters of 221 words – with every chapter ending with a word that starts with B.

THE ADVENTURE OF THE COLONIAL BOY
BY NARRELLE M HARRIS

It's 1893, and Dr John Watson, still mourning his friend after his death at the Reichenbach Falls, is now triply bereaved by his wife Mary's death in childbirth. Then a telegram from Australia interrupts his grief: *Come at once if convenient.*

Desperate to believe Holmes may still be alive, Watson takes an unexpectedly dangerous voyage to the Australian colony of Victoria.

And soon Holmes and Watson are racing through bohemian Melbourne, tackling a series of murders linked to a red leech and a remnant of Moriarty's gang. But things are not as they were.

Can Sherlock Holmes and Dr Watson solve a crime, save a life, rediscover trust…and admit to love?

A Murmuring of Bees
edited by Atlin Merrick

Think of Sherlock Holmes and you think of
mysteries, John Watson, and bees.

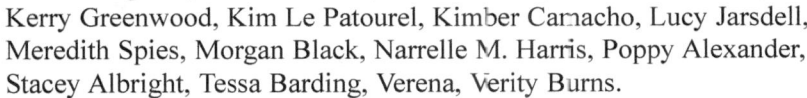

Here bees are front and centre in tales of secret
diaries, rare nectars, and the private language of
lovers, where John and Sherlock are helping one
another, romancing one another, *loving one* another.

Contributors:

Amy L Webb, Anarion, Atlin Merrick,
Brittany Russ, Darcy Lindbergh, Elinor Gray,
Hallie Deighton, Jamie Ashbird, Janet A-Nunn,
Kerry Greenwood, Kim Le Patourel, Kimber Camacho, Lucy Jarsdell,
Meredith Spies, Morgan Black, Narrelle M. Harris, Poppy Alexander,
Stacey Albright, Tessa Barding, Verena, Verity Burns.

> To encourage a world where such love is seen as the precious thing it is,
> profits from *A Murmuring of Bees* are donated to the It Gets Better Project.

Sherlock Holmes and John Watson: The Night They Met
by Atlin Merrick

Some things belong together, the one with the
other, natural pairs.

Sherlock Holmes and John Watson.

Whether it's in an empty house during the
Blitz, a West London strip club in the 70s, or
deep in the heart of a Hong Kong computer
lab, the meeting of these two legendary men
is inevitable.

Spanning 128 years, here are 19 stories of
that destiny: of how, no matter where they are
or when, a detective meets a doctor; of how
they change each other in heart and mind; of
how they fall in love.

Sign up for *Spark!*
The free newsletter on writing from Improbable Press.
spark-by-improbable-press.tumblr.com